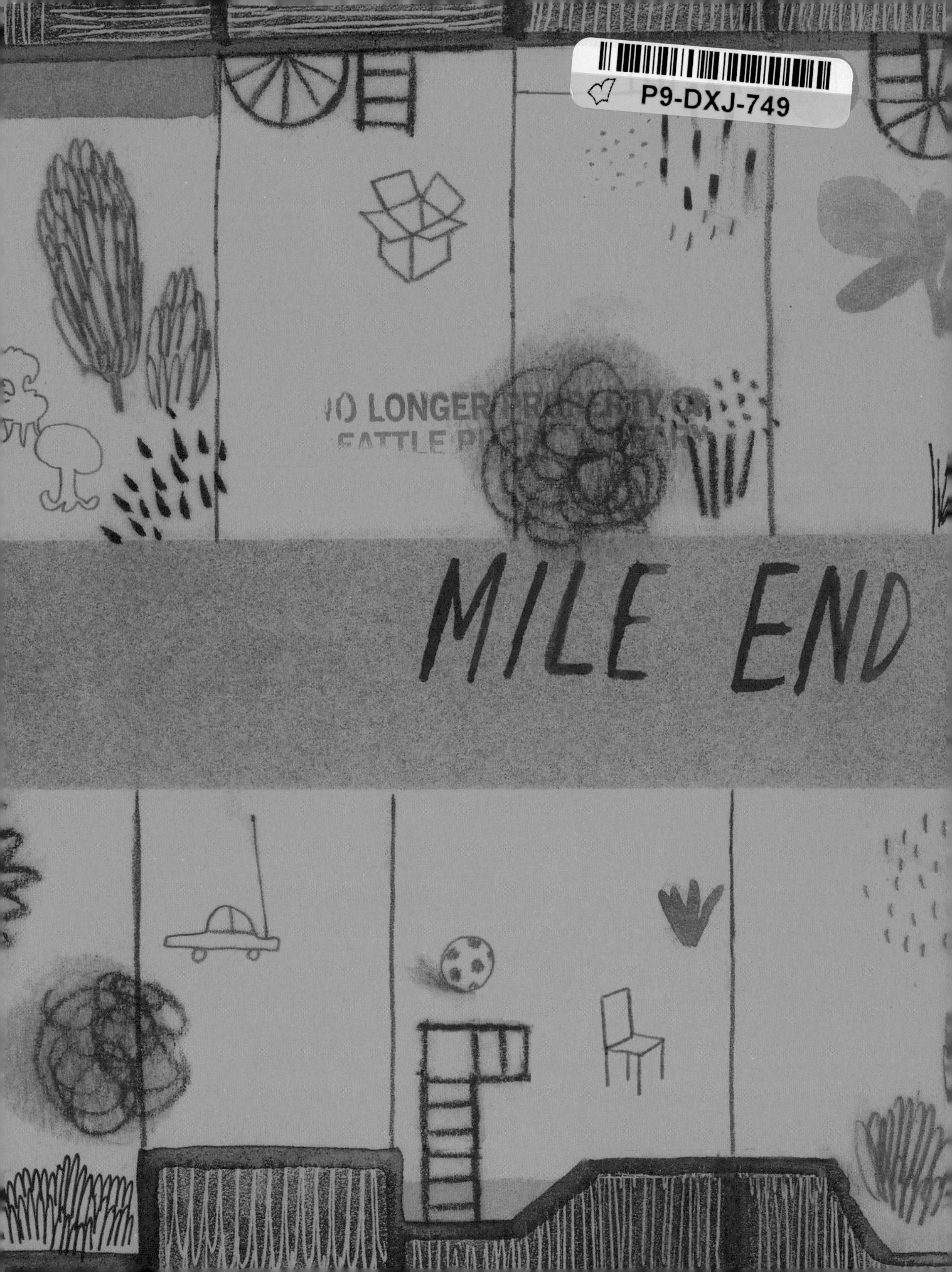
MILE END

In memory of my dear friend Valérie,
queen of life with confetti

Tundra Books, an imprint of Penguin Random House Canada Young Readers, a division of
Penguin Random House of Canada Limited

Library and Archives Canada Cataloguing in Publication

Title: Maya's big scene / Isabelle Arsenault.
Names: Arsenault, Isabelle, 1978– author.
Identifiers: Canadiana (print) 20200182161 | Canadiana (ebook) 2020018217X | ISBN 9780735267602
     (hardcover) | ISBN 9780735267619 (EPUB)
Classification: LCC PS8601R7538 M39 2021 | DDC jC813/.6—dc23

Published simultaneously in the United States of America by Tundra Books of Northern New
York, an imprint of Penguin Random House Canada Young Readers, a division of Penguin
Random House of Canada Limited

Library of Congress Control Number: 2020936475

Edited by Tara Walker with assistance from Margot Blankier
Designed by Isabelle Arsenault and Kelly Hill
The artwork in this book was rendered in pencils, watercolor and ink
with digital coloration in Photoshop.
Handlettering by Isabelle Arsenault.

Printed and bound in China

Canada Council   Conseil des arts
for the Arts   du Canada

We acknowledge the support of the Canada Council for the Arts.

www.penguinrandomhouse.ca

1   2   3   4   5   25   24   23   22   21

Penguin
Random House
tundra | TUNDRA BOOKS

A Mile End Kids Story

MAYA'S BIG SCENE

Words and pictures by
ISABELLE ARSENAULT

TUNDRA

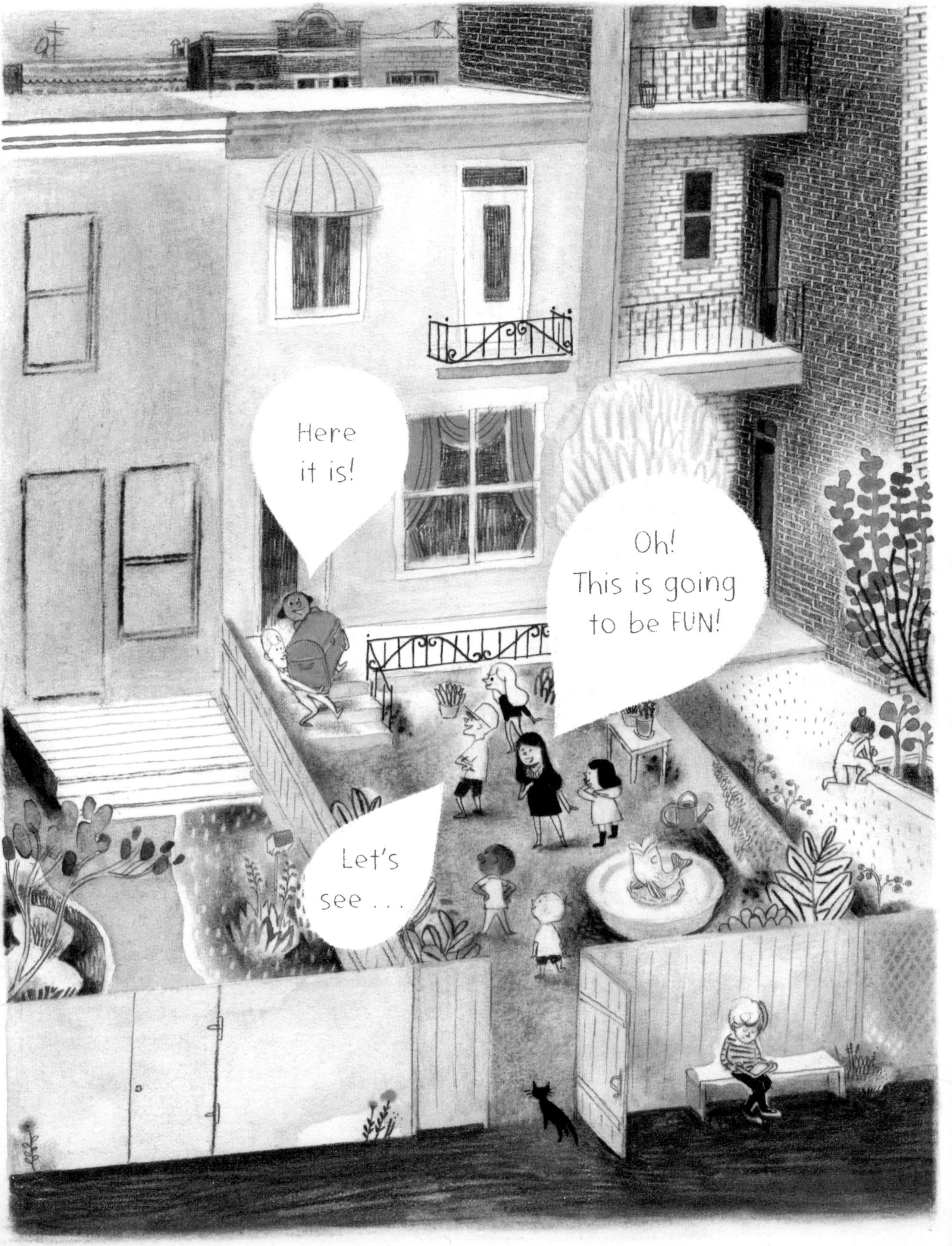
Here it is!
Oh! This is going to be FUN!
Let's see . . .

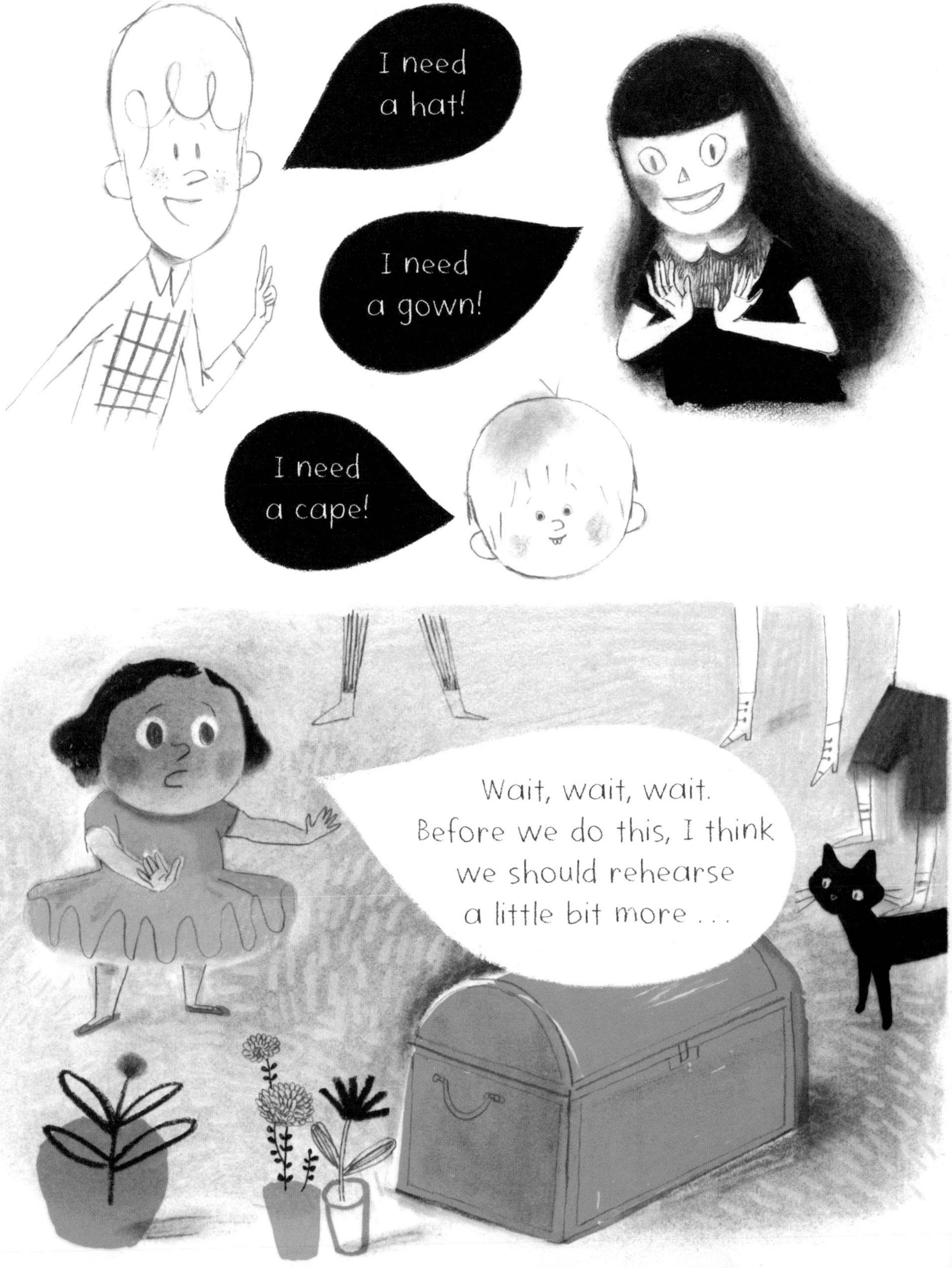
I need a hat!
I need a gown!
I need a cape!
Wait, wait, wait. Before we do this, I think we should rehearse a little bit more . . .

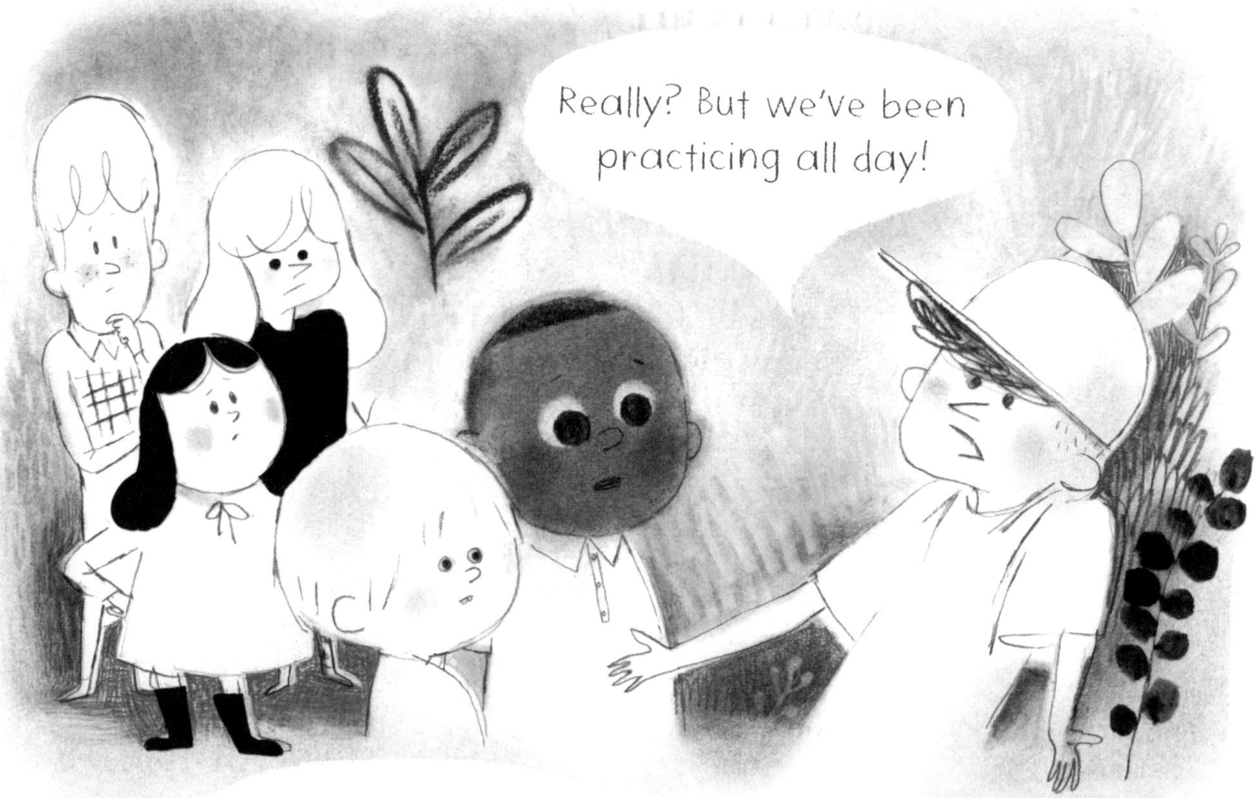
Really? But we've been practicing all day!

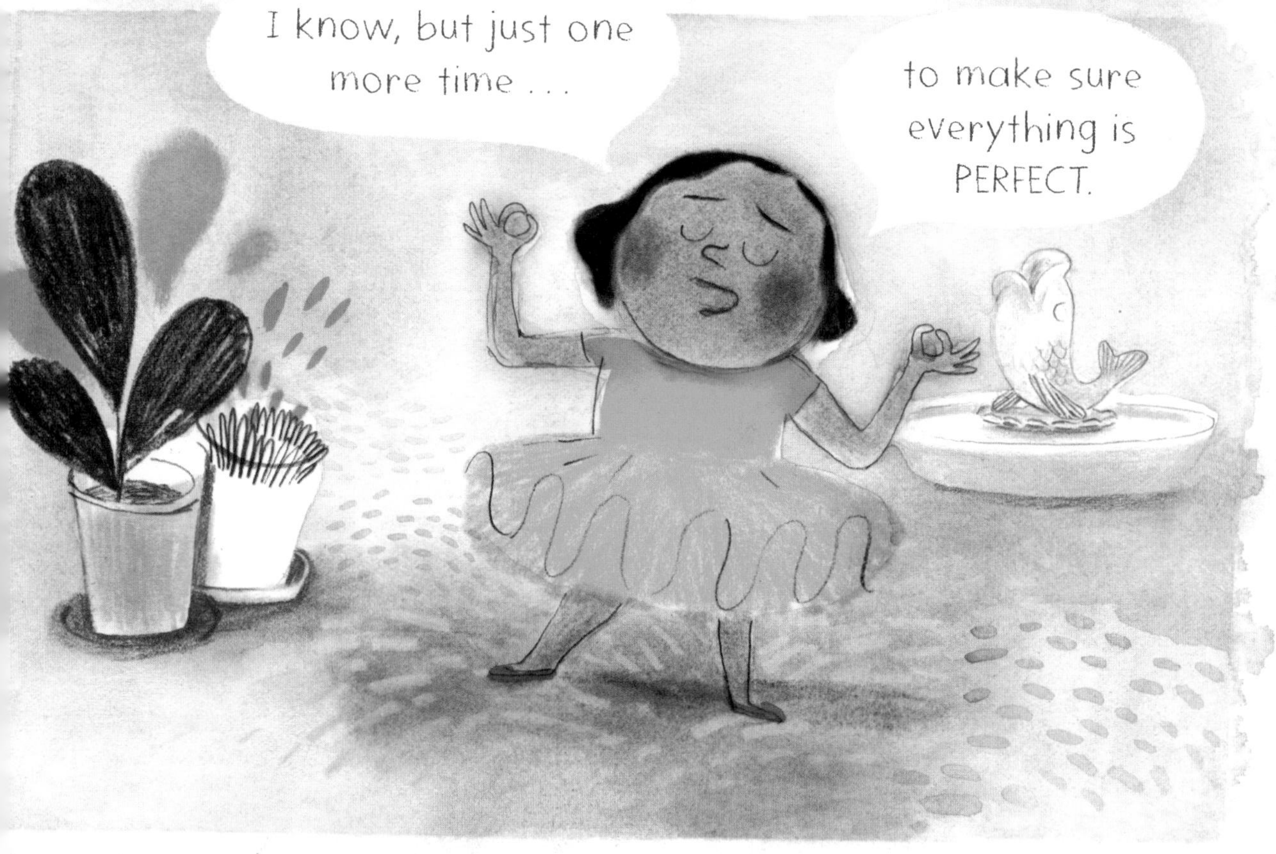
I know, but just one more time . . .
to make sure everything is PERFECT.

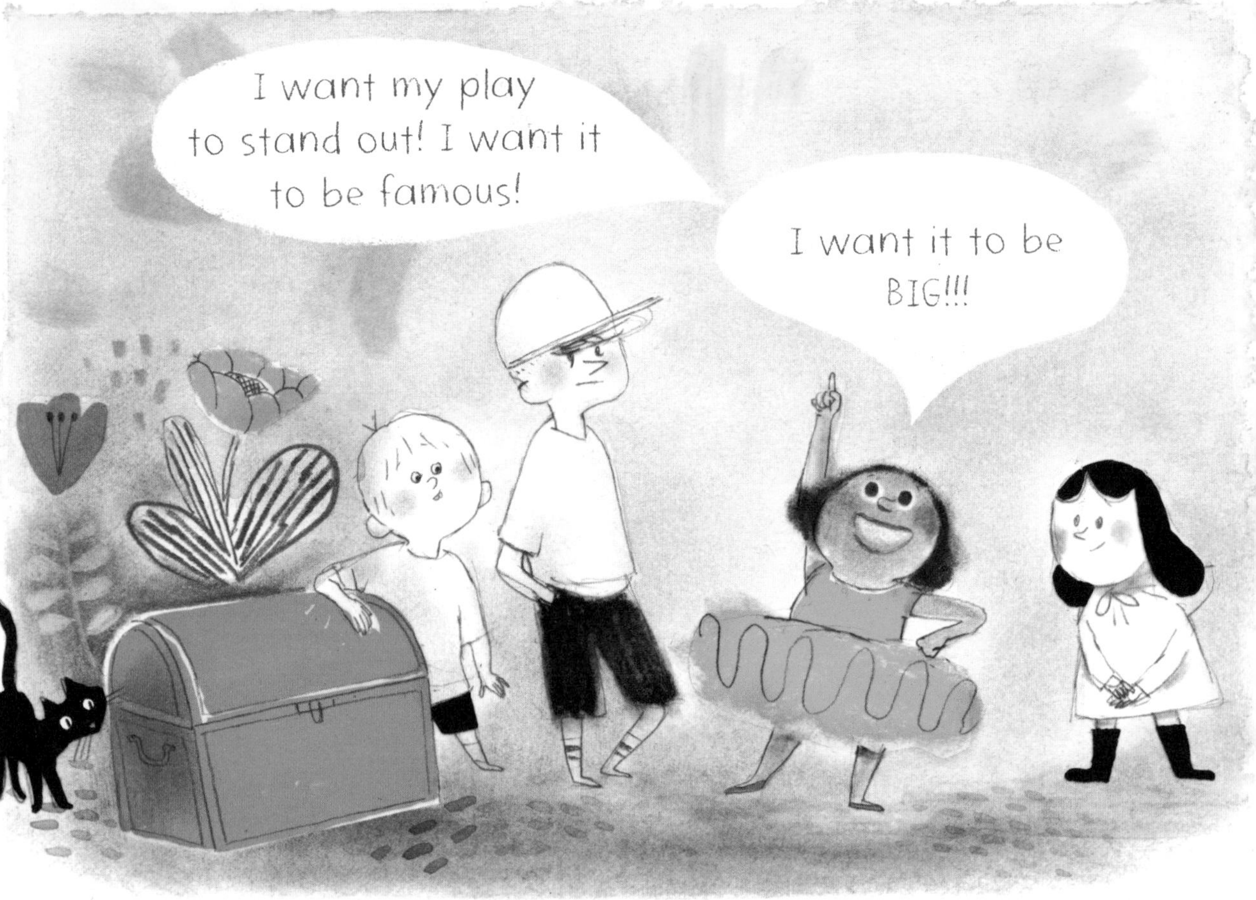
I want my play to stand out! I want it to be famous!
I want it to be BIG!!!

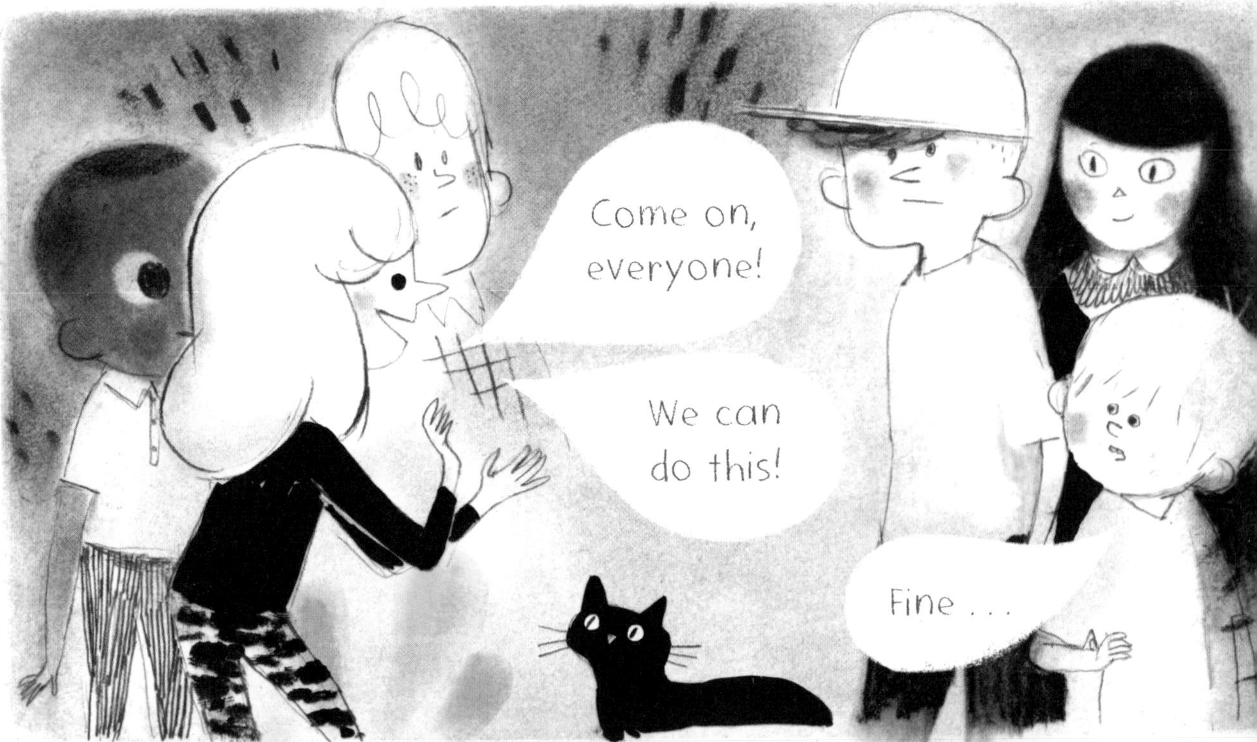
Come on, everyone!
We can do this!
Fine . . .

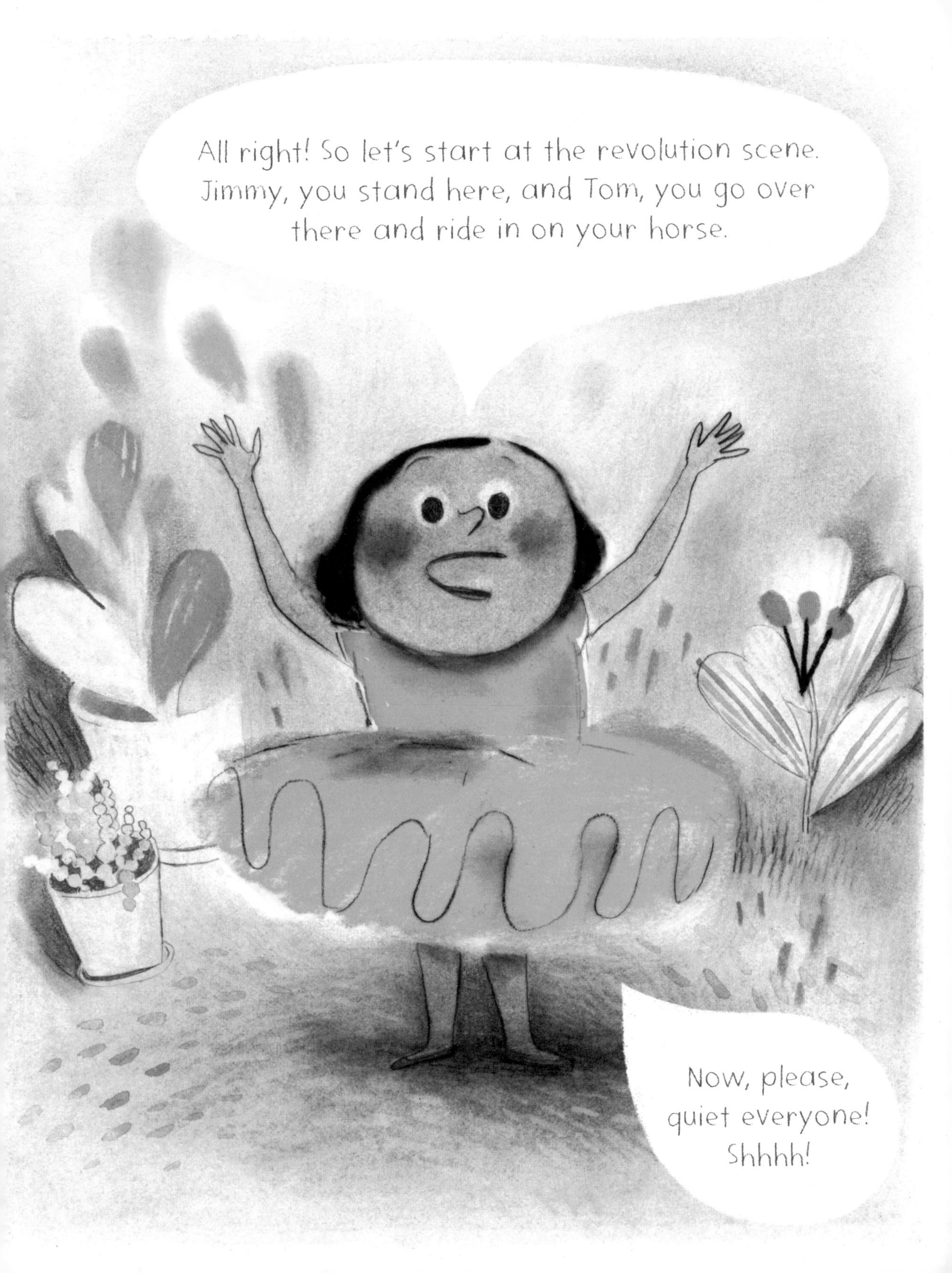
All right! So let's start at the revolution scene. Jimmy, you stand here, and Tom, you go over there and ride in on your horse.
Now, please, quiet everyone! Shhhh!

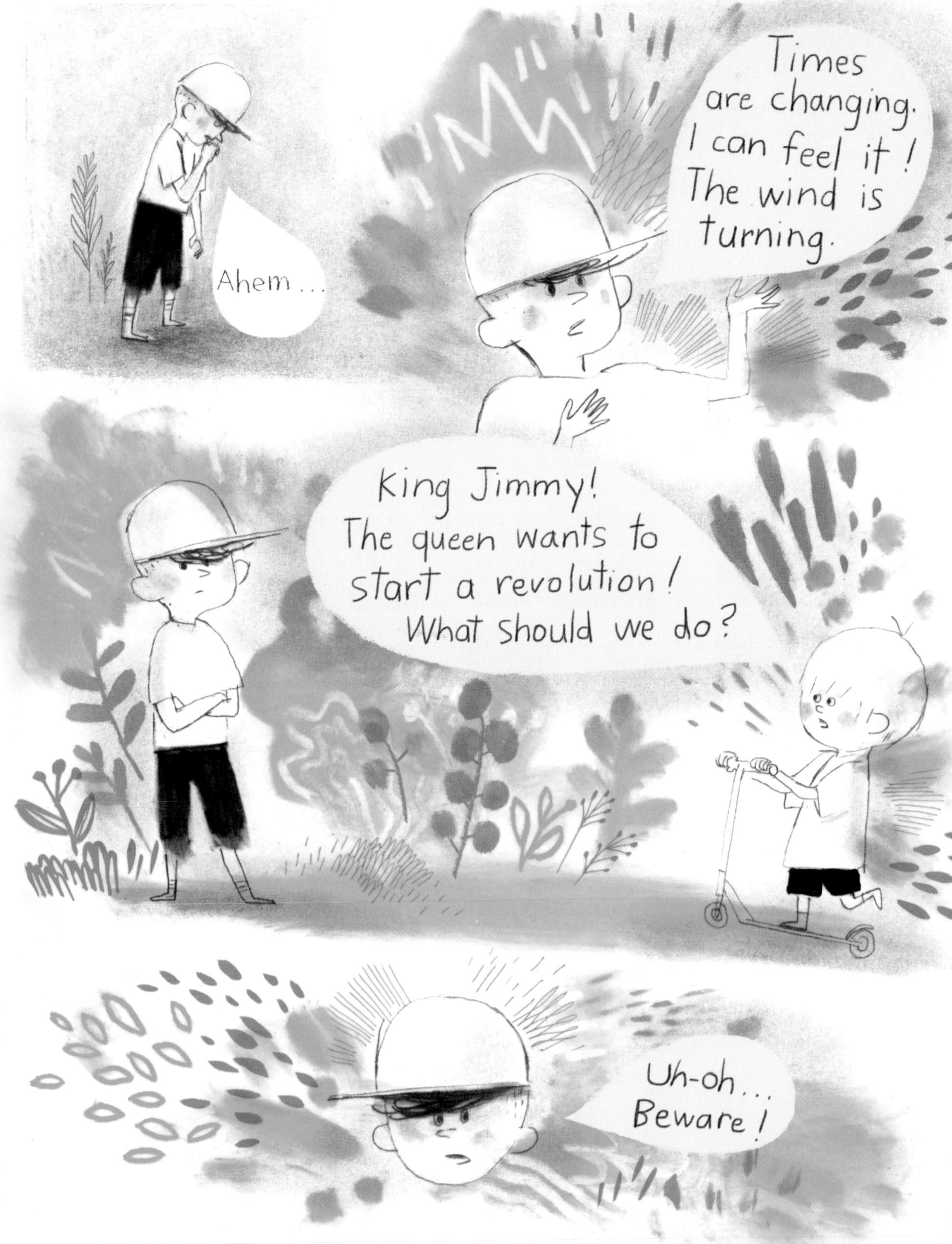
Ahem ...
Times are changing. I can feel it! The wind is turning.
King Jimmy! The queen wants to start a revolution! What should we do?
Uh-oh... Beware!

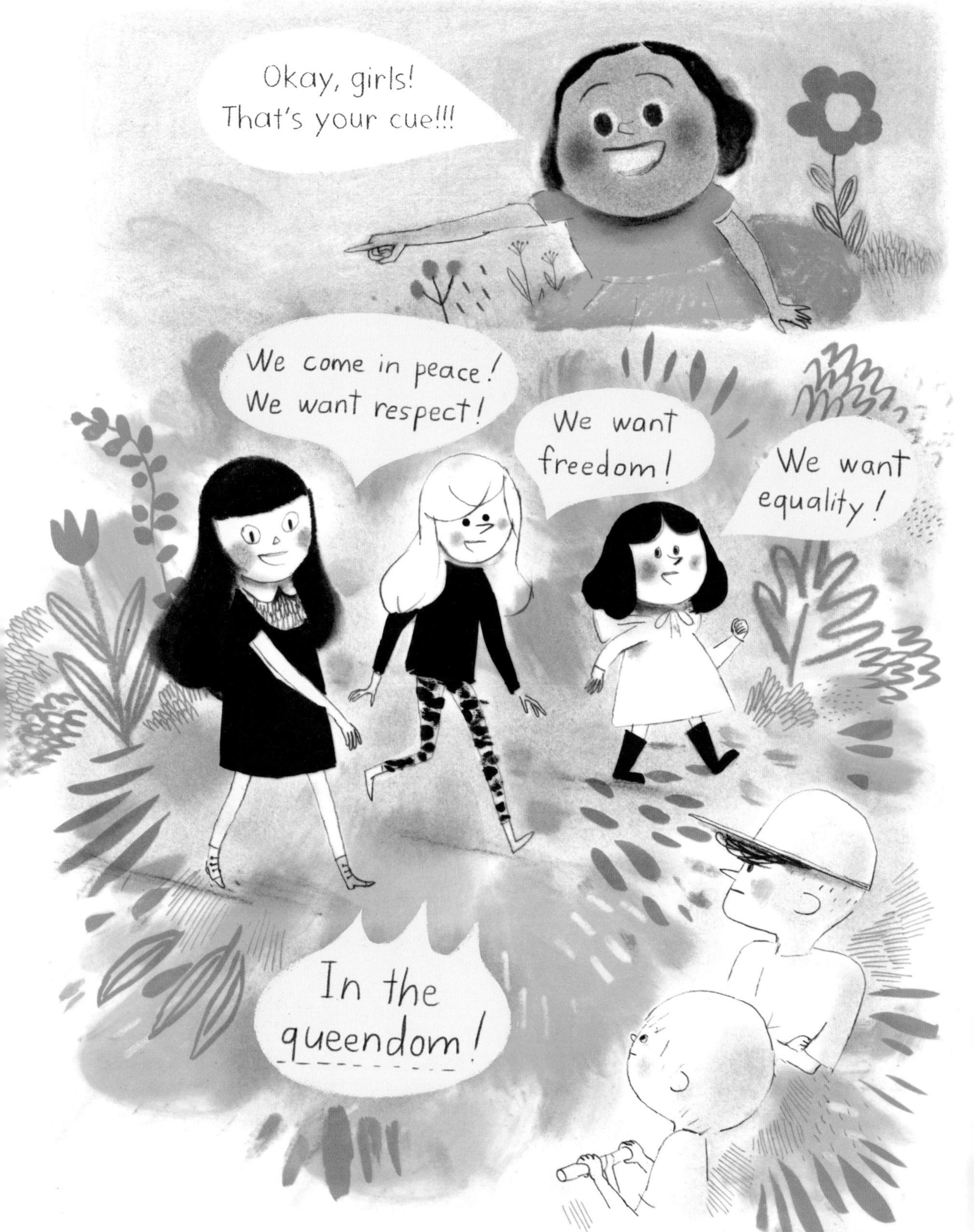
Okay, girls! That's your cue!!!
We come in peace! We want respect!
We want freedom!
We want equality!
In the queendom!

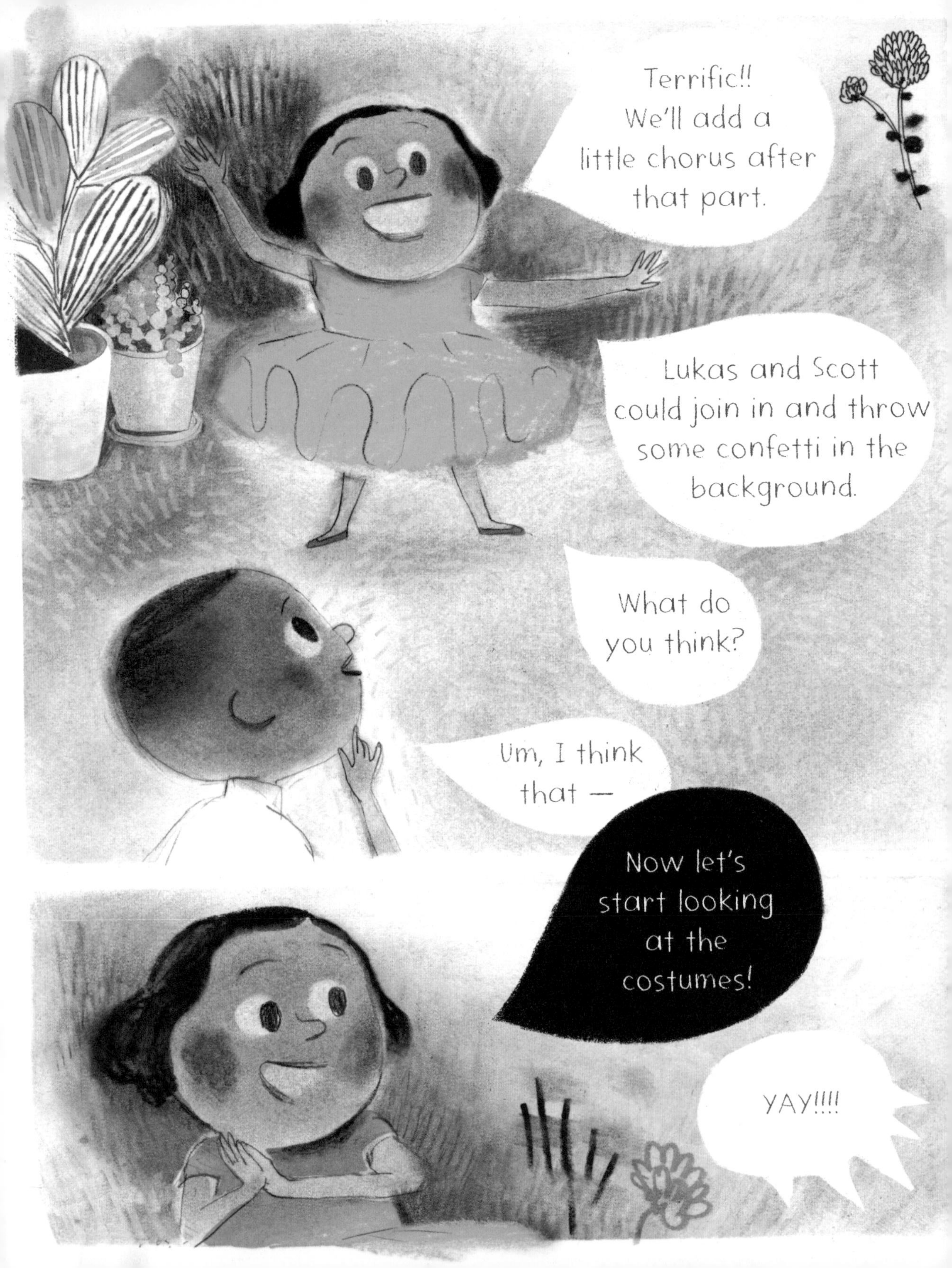
Terrific!! We'll add a little chorus after that part.
Lukas and Scott could join in and throw some confetti in the background.
What do you think?
Um, I think that —
Now let's start looking at the costumes!
YAY!!!!

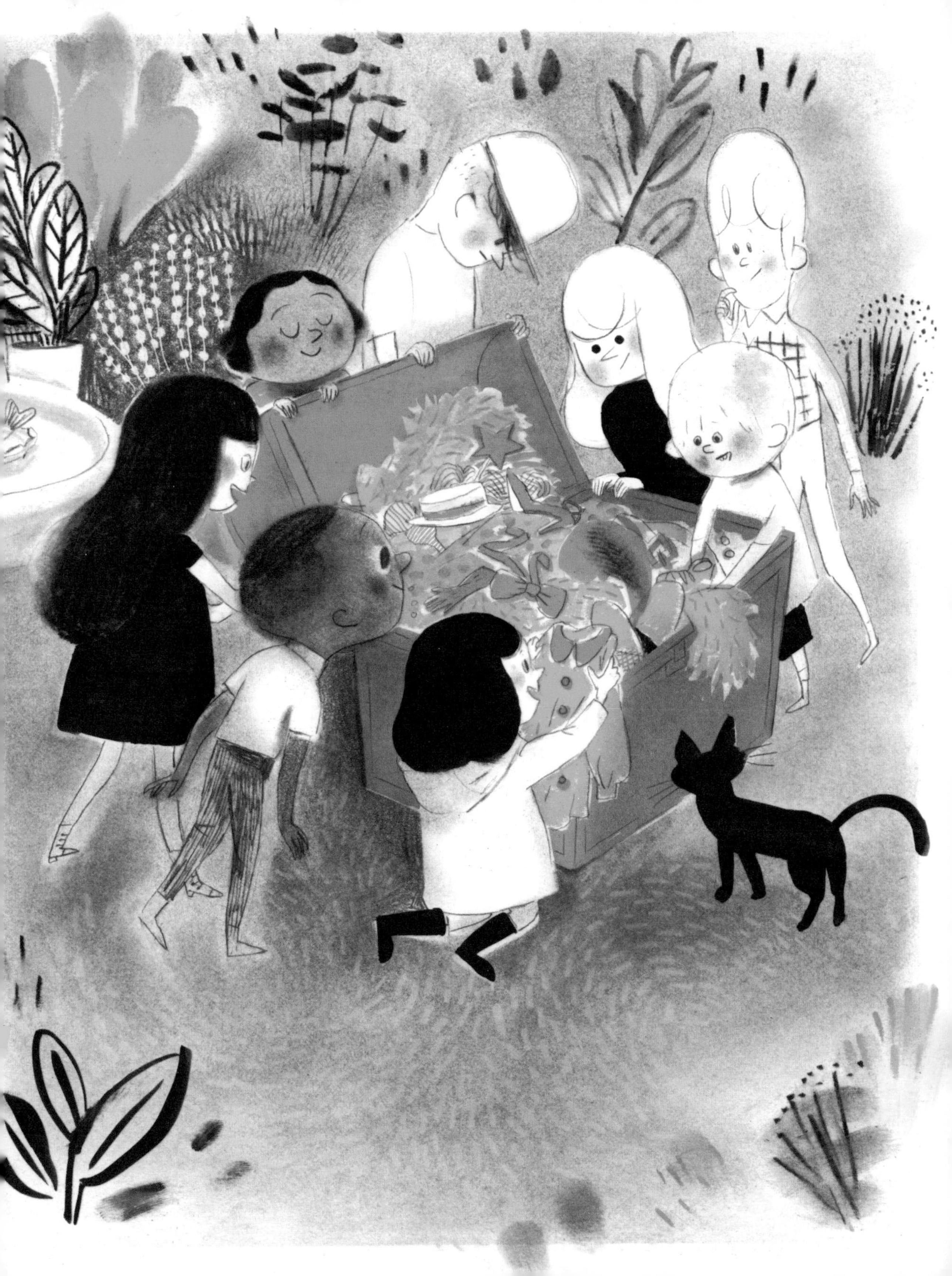

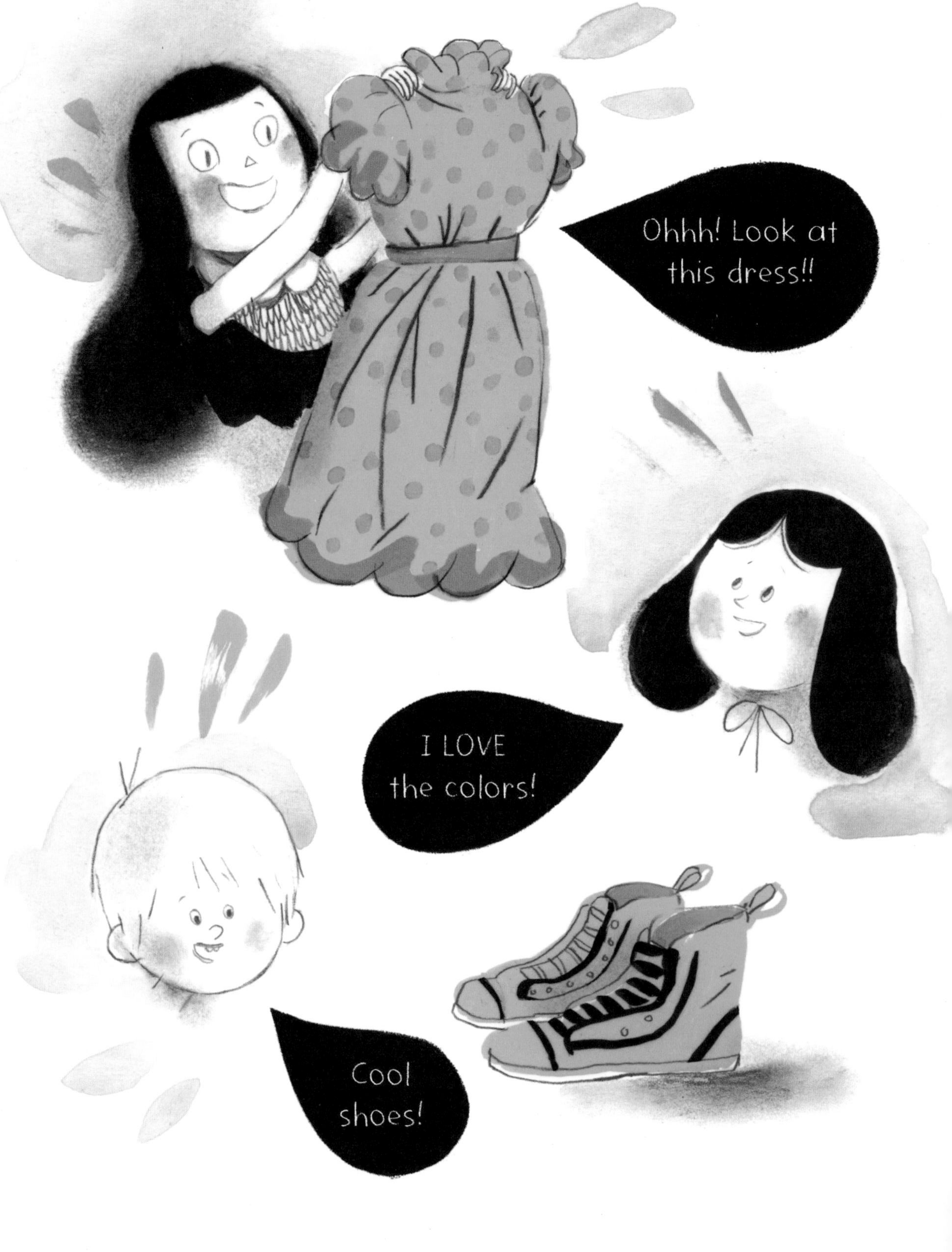
Ohhh! Look at this dress!!
I LOVE the colors!
Cool shoes!

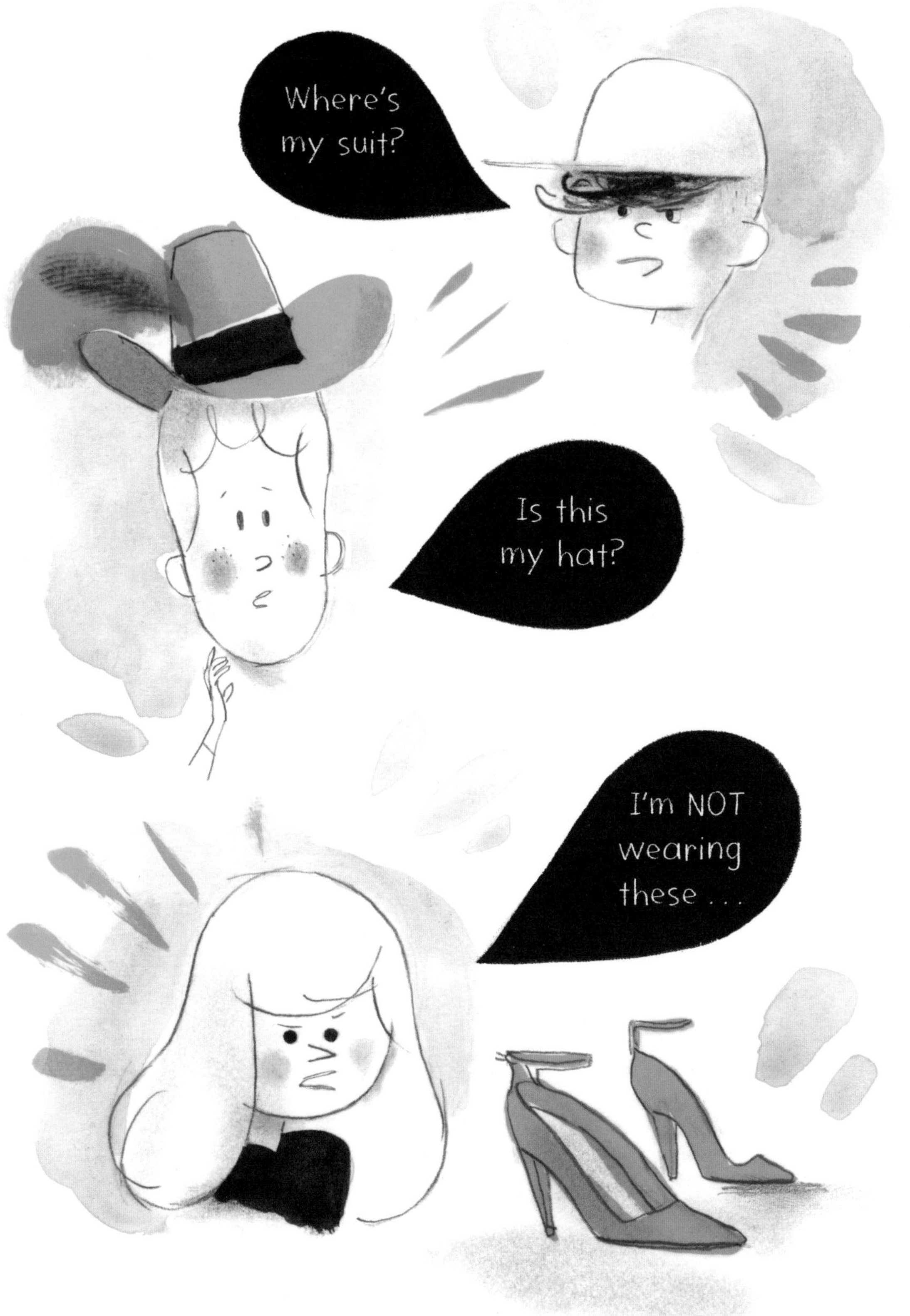
Where's my suit?
Is this my hat?
I'm NOT wearing these . . .

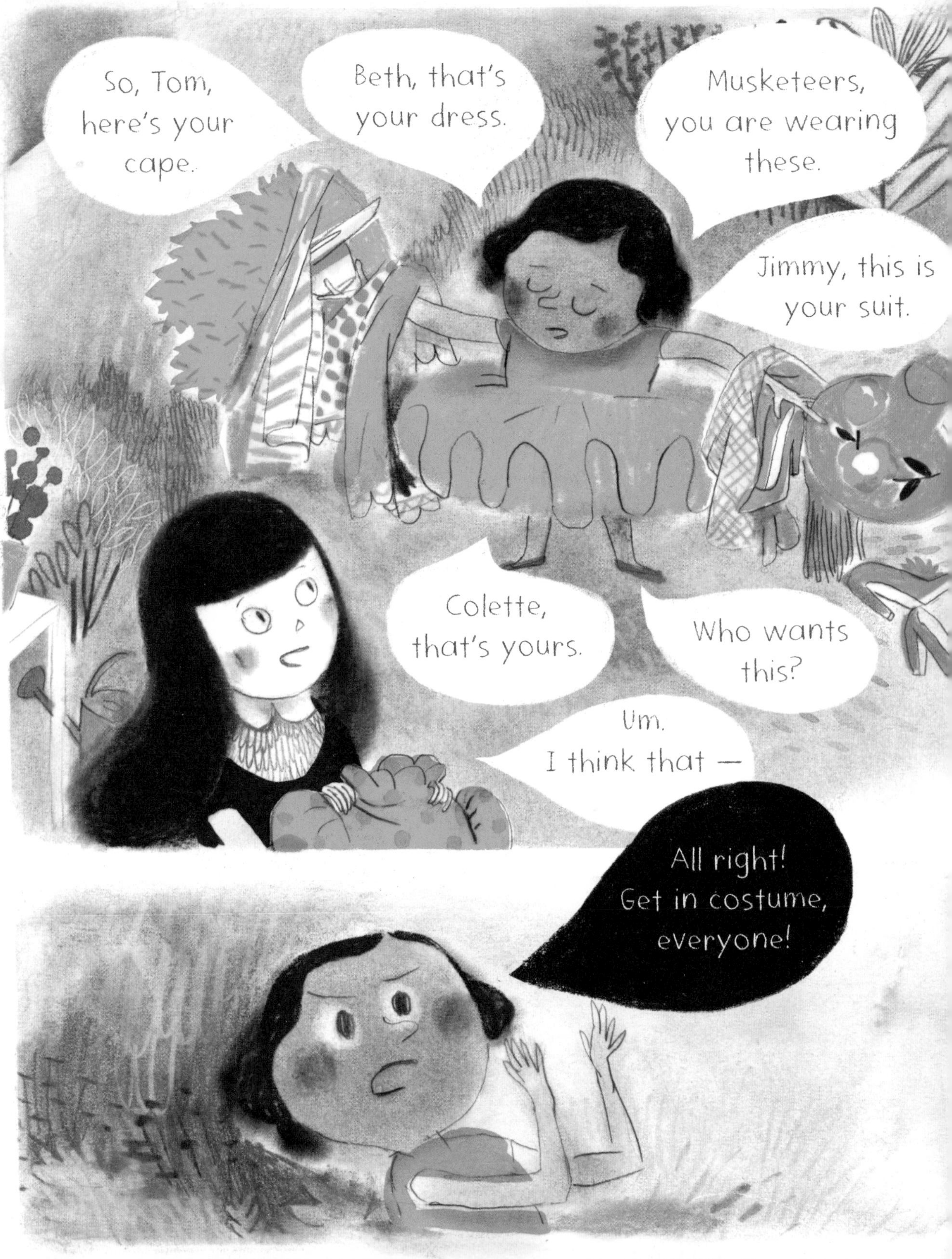
So, Tom, here's your cape.
Beth, that's your dress.
Musketeers, you are wearing these.
Jimmy, this is your suit.
Colette, that's yours.
Who wants this?
Um. I think that —
All right! Get in costume, everyone!

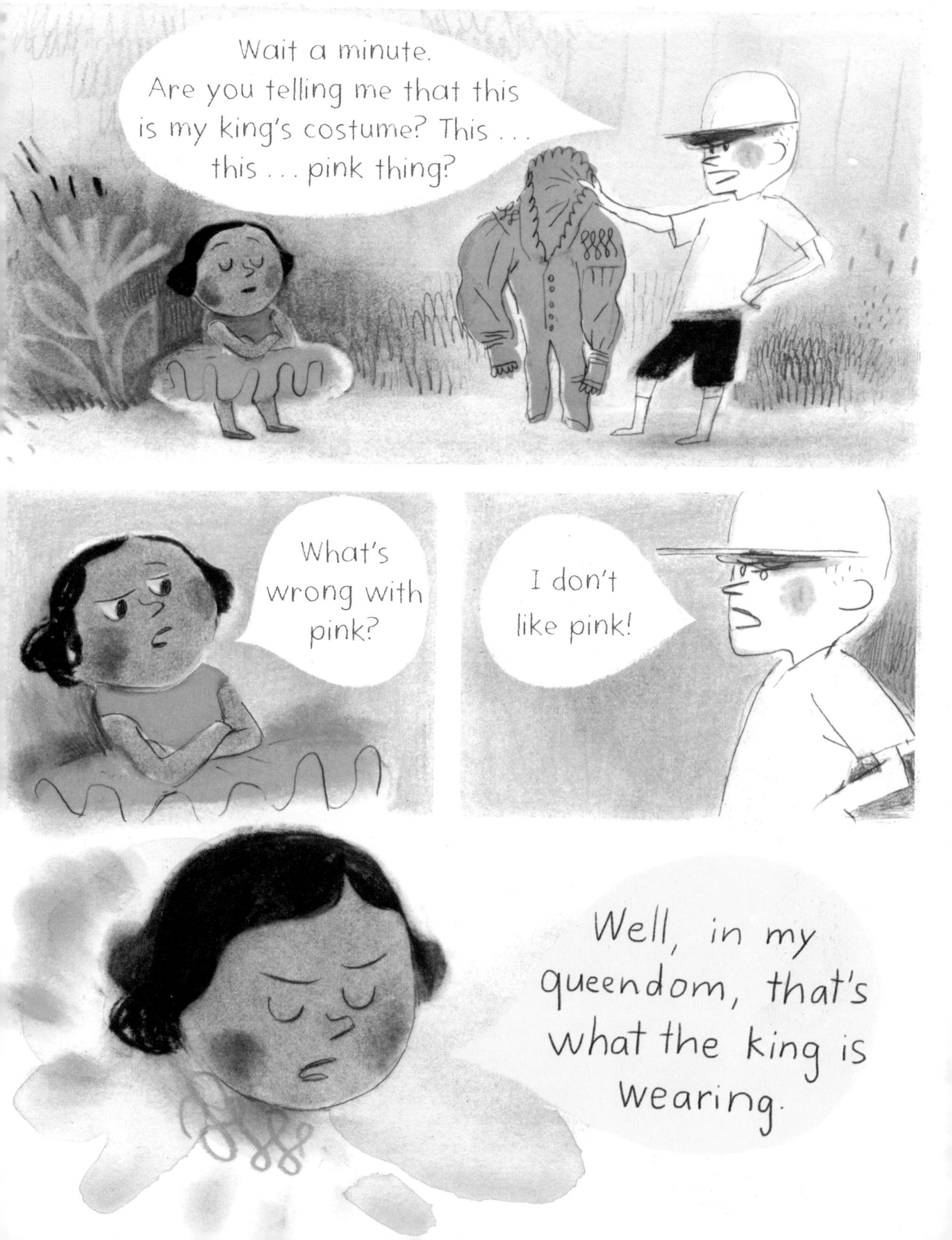

Wait a minute. Are you telling me that this is my king's costume? This . . . this . . . pink thing?
What's wrong with pink?
I don't like pink!
Well, in my queendom, that's what the king is wearing.

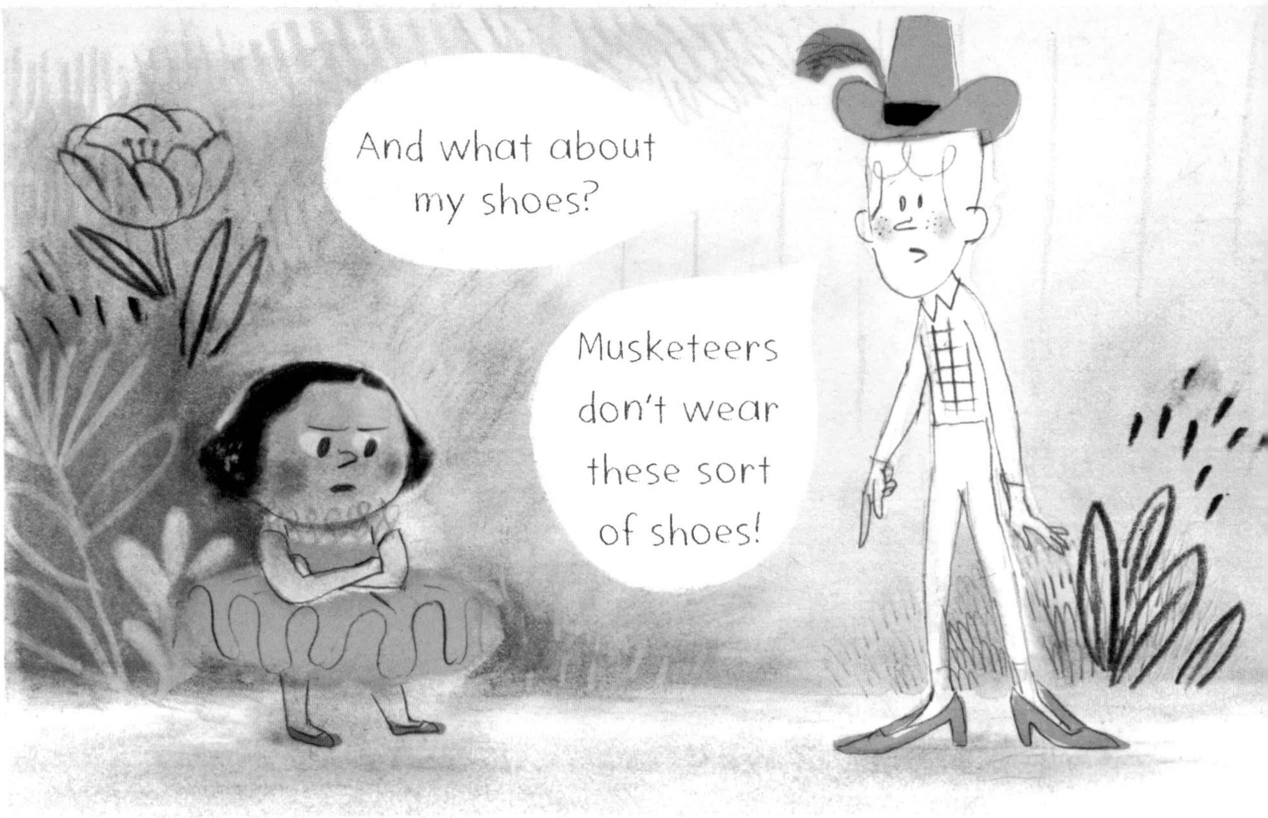
And what about my shoes?
Musketeers don't wear these sort of shoes!

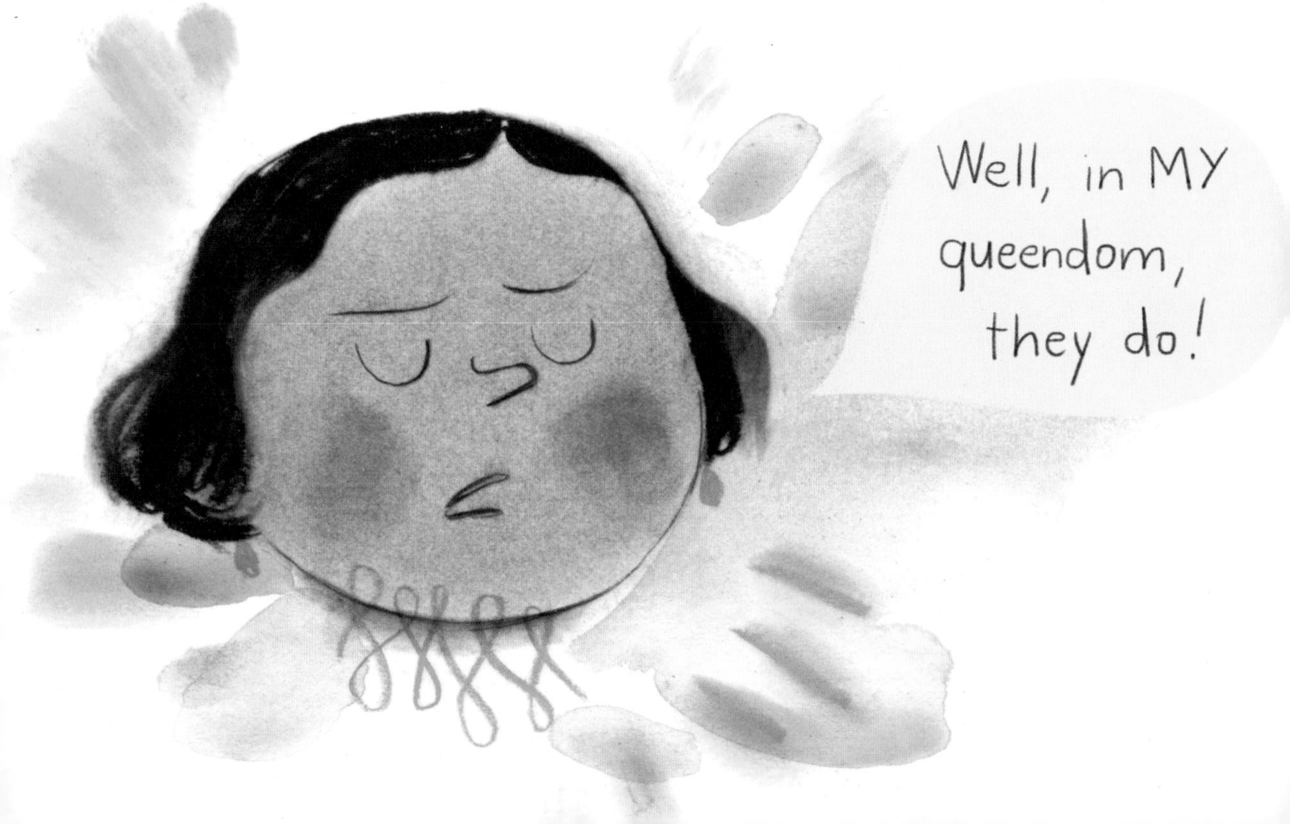
Well, in MY queendom, they do!

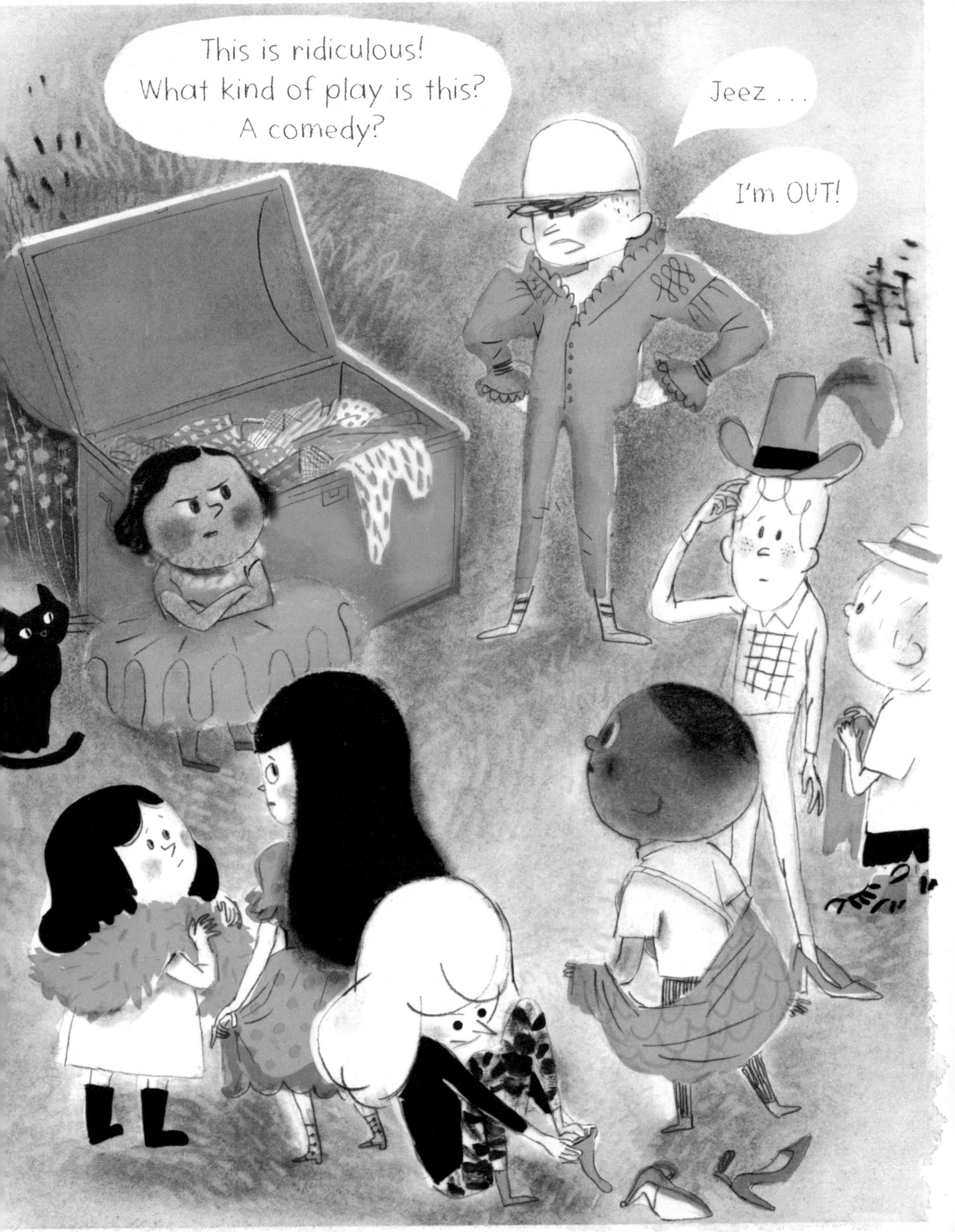
This is ridiculous! What kind of play is this? A comedy?
Jeez . . .
I'm OUT!

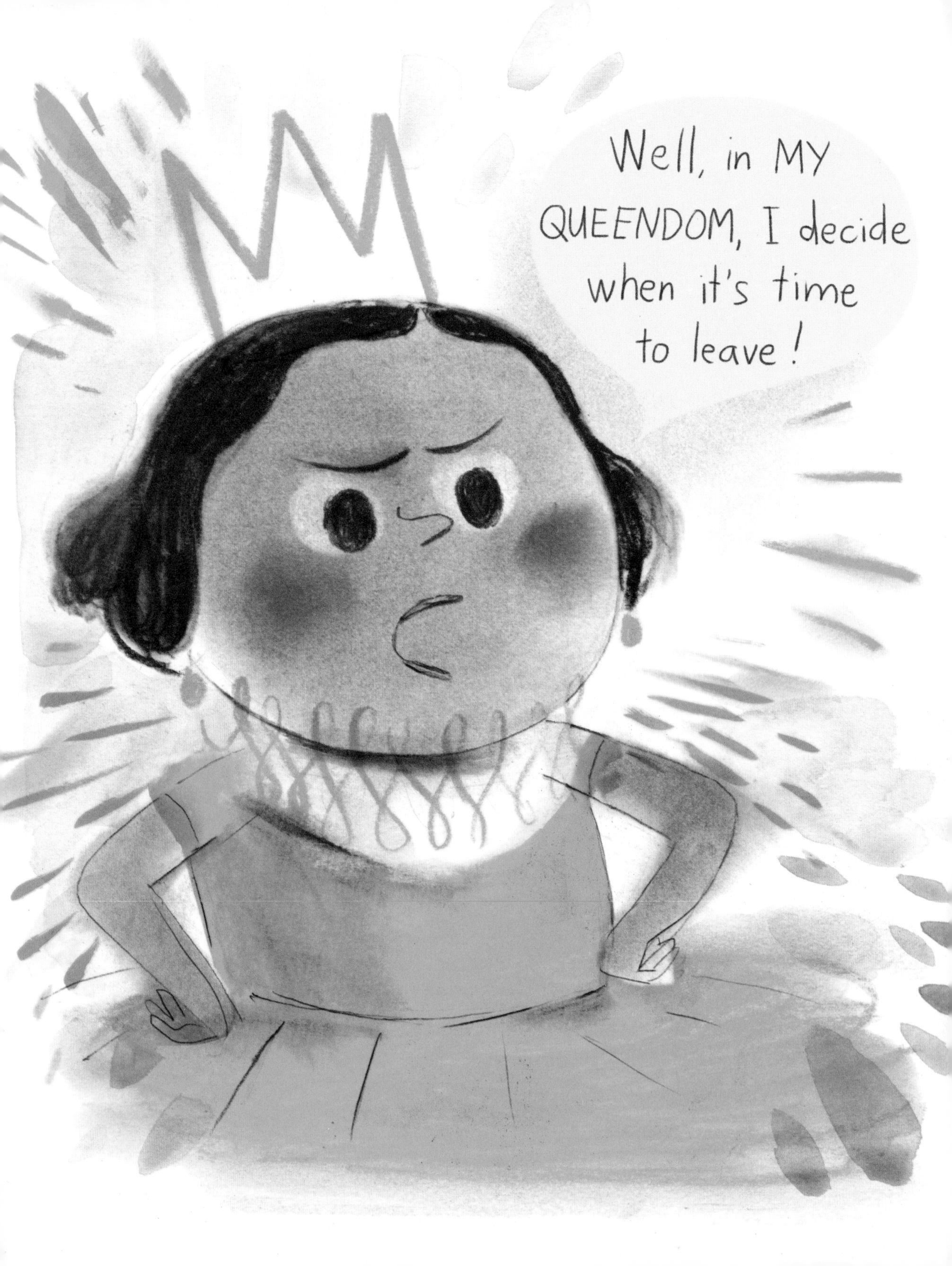
Well, in MY QUEENDOM, I decide when it's time to leave!

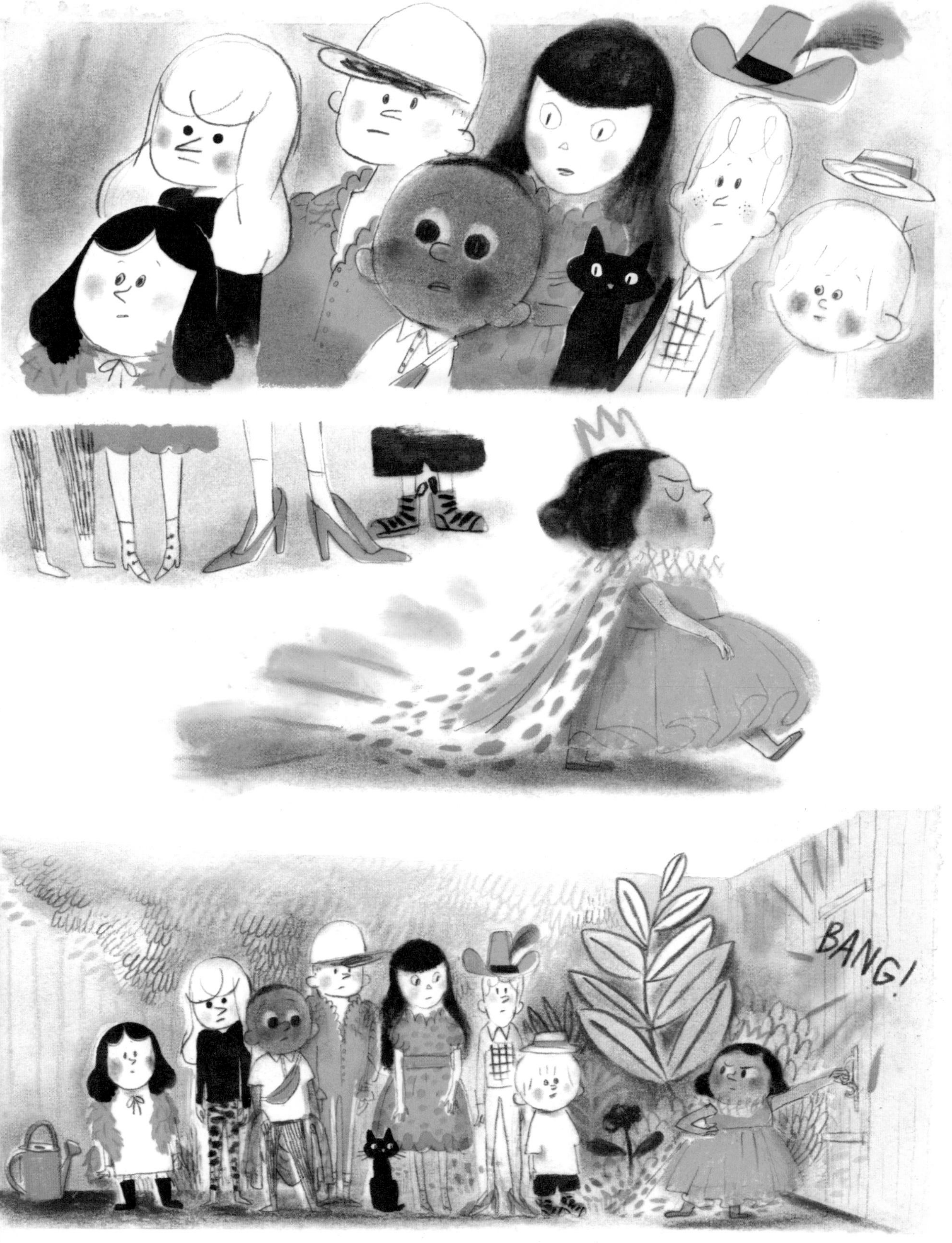
BANG!

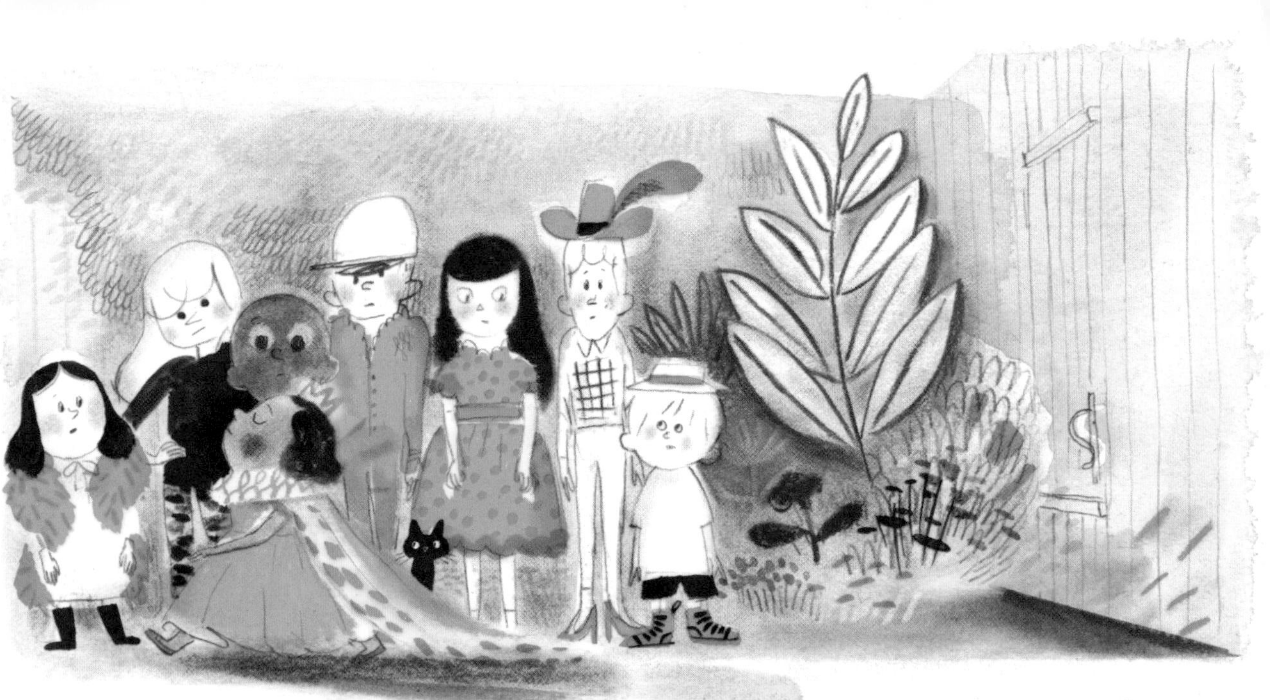

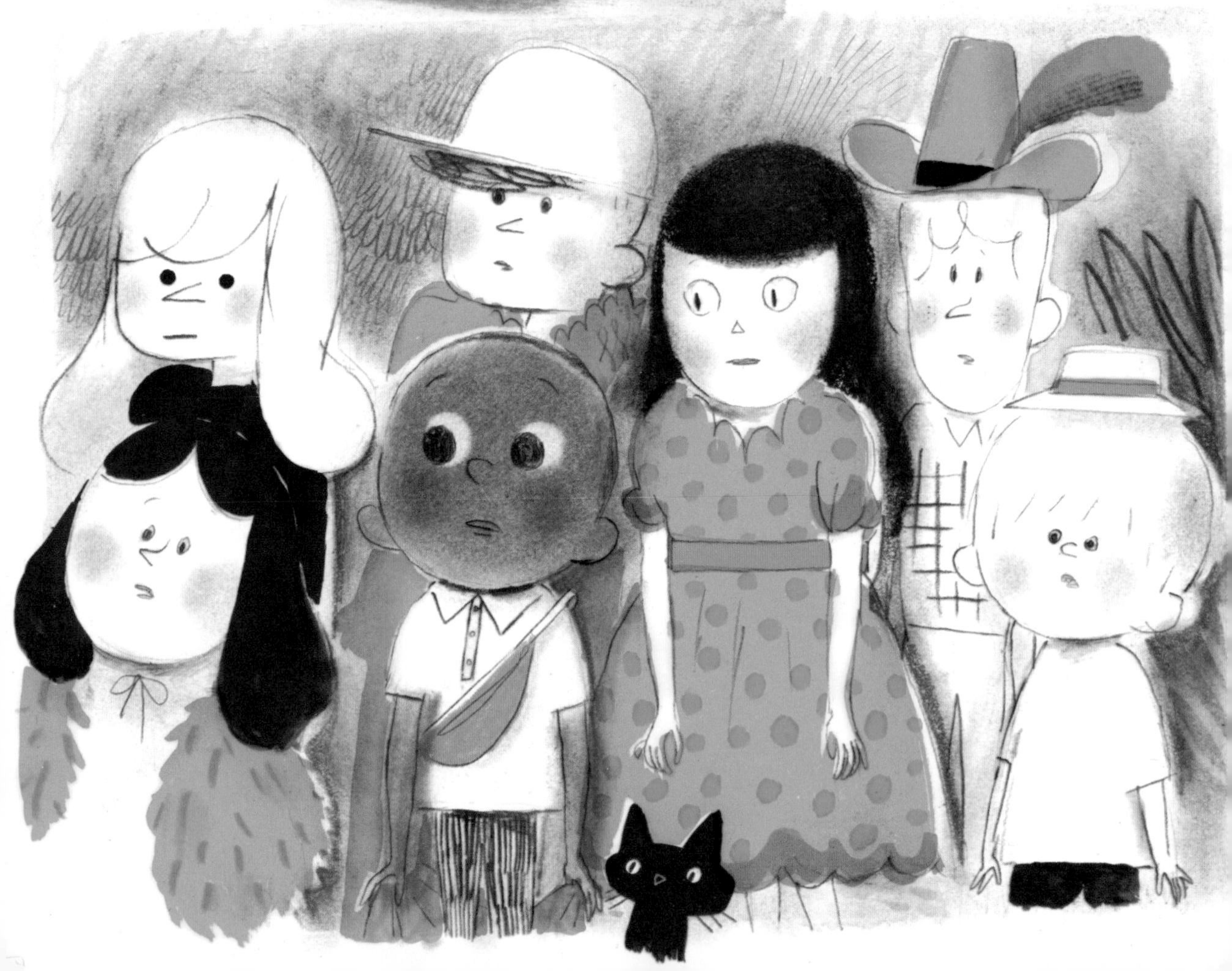

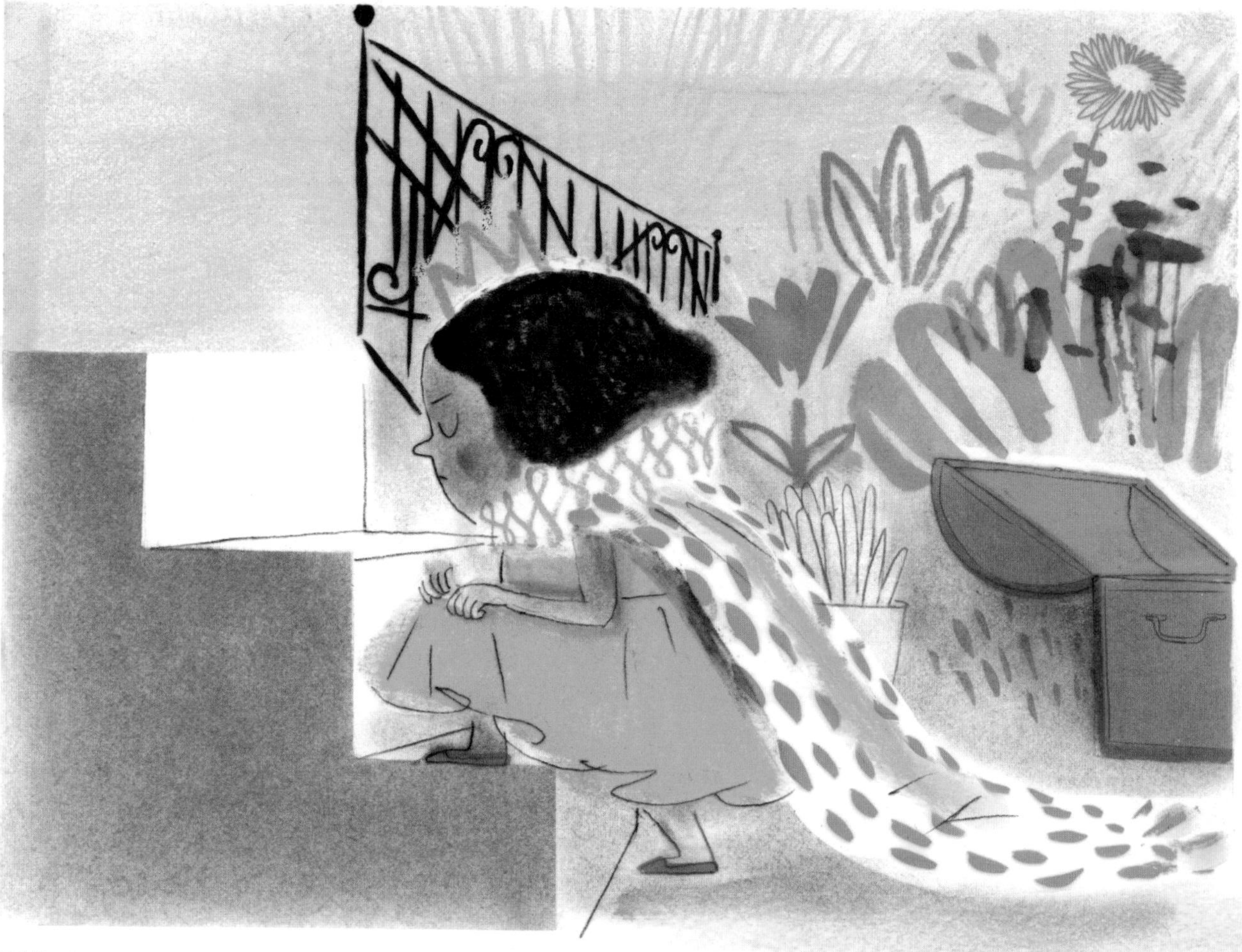

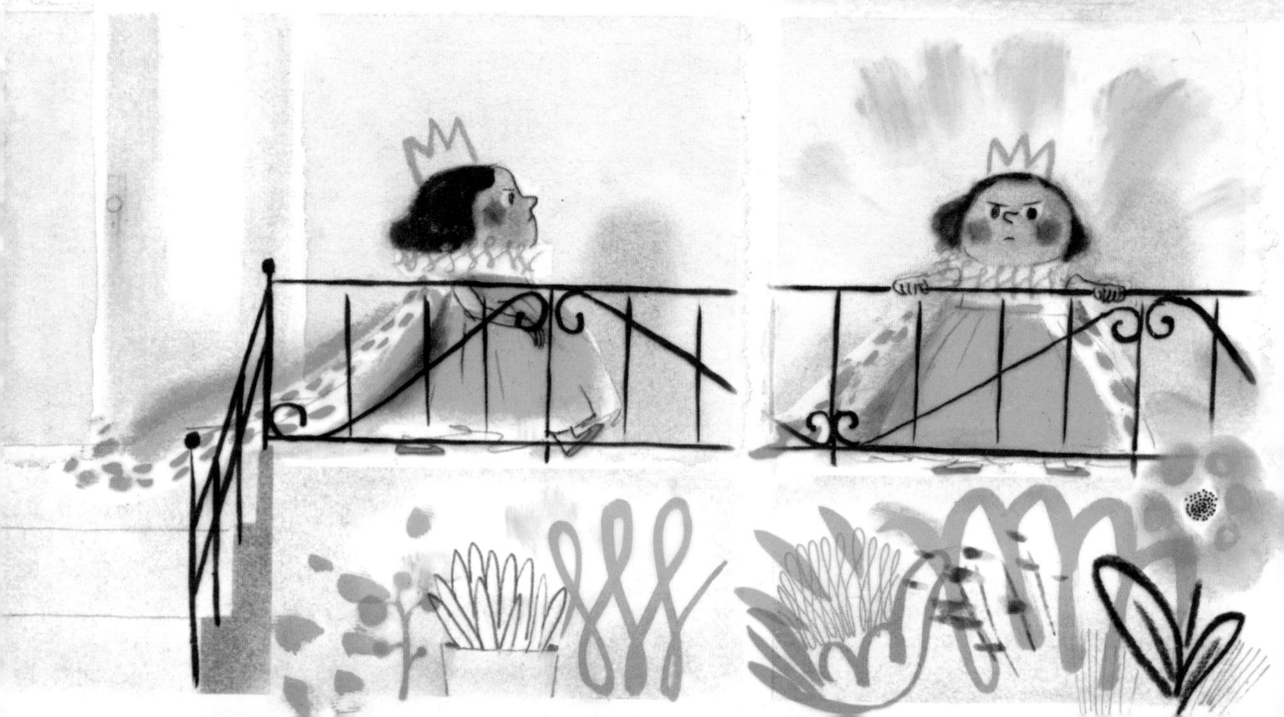

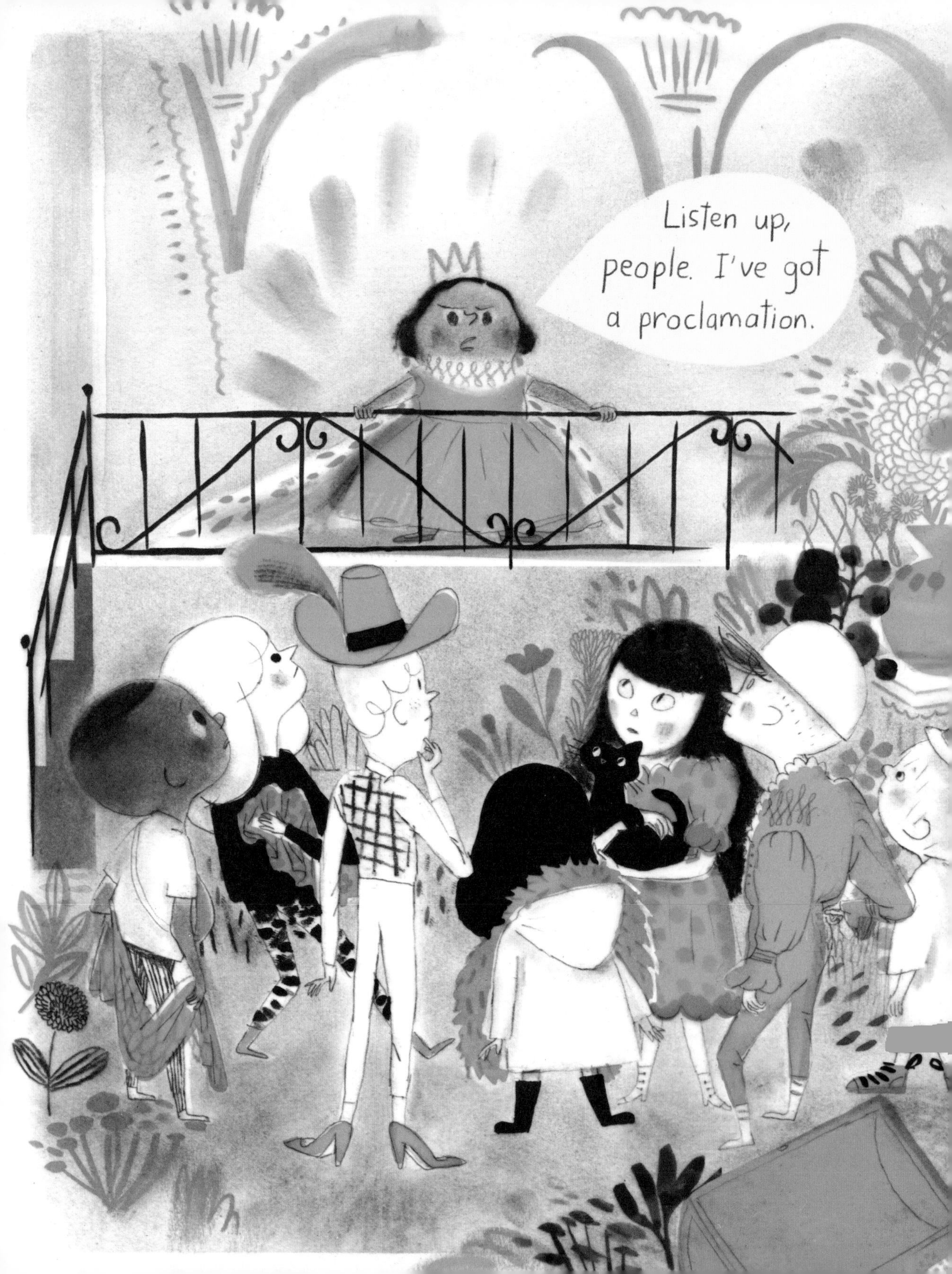
Listen up, people. I've got a proclamation.

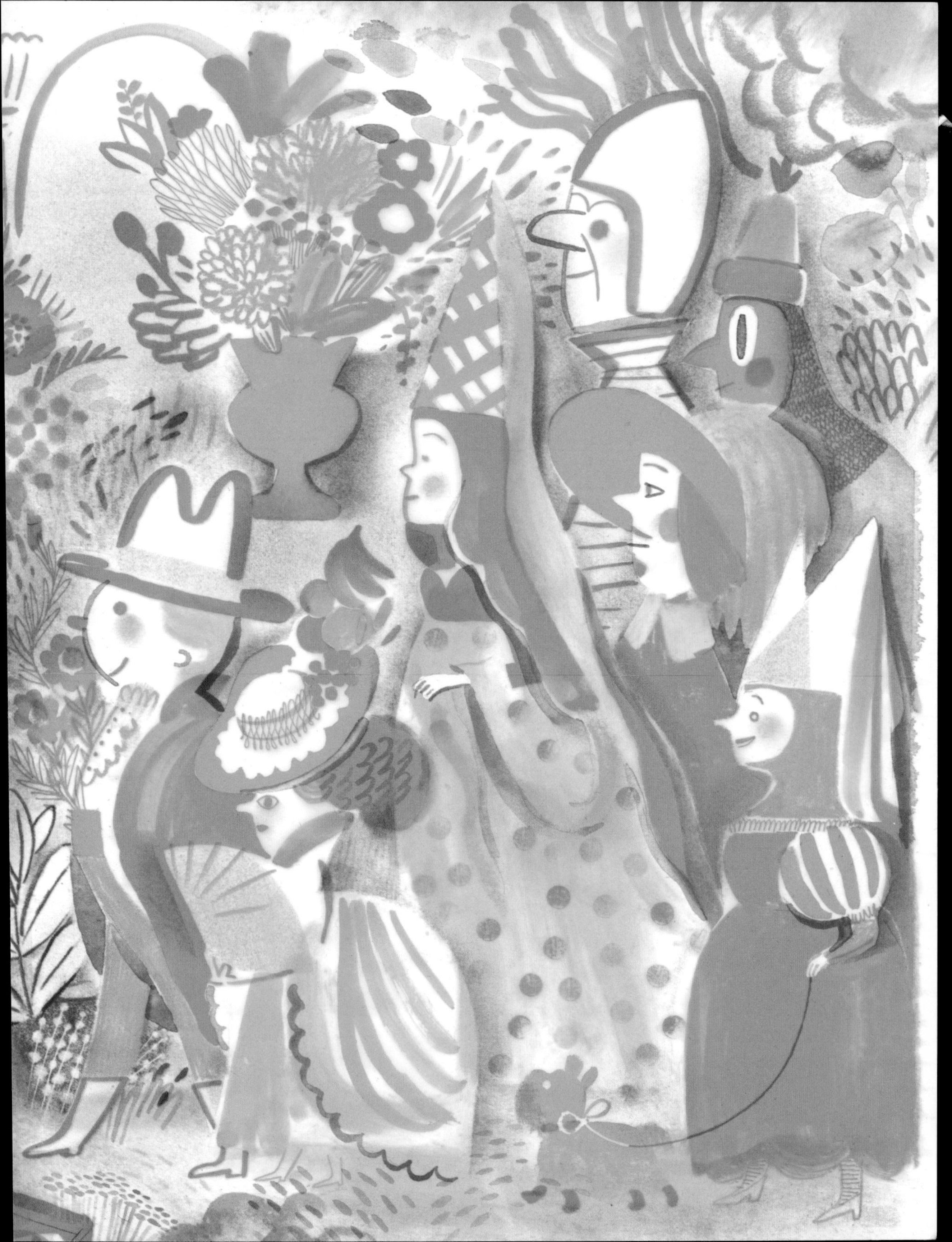

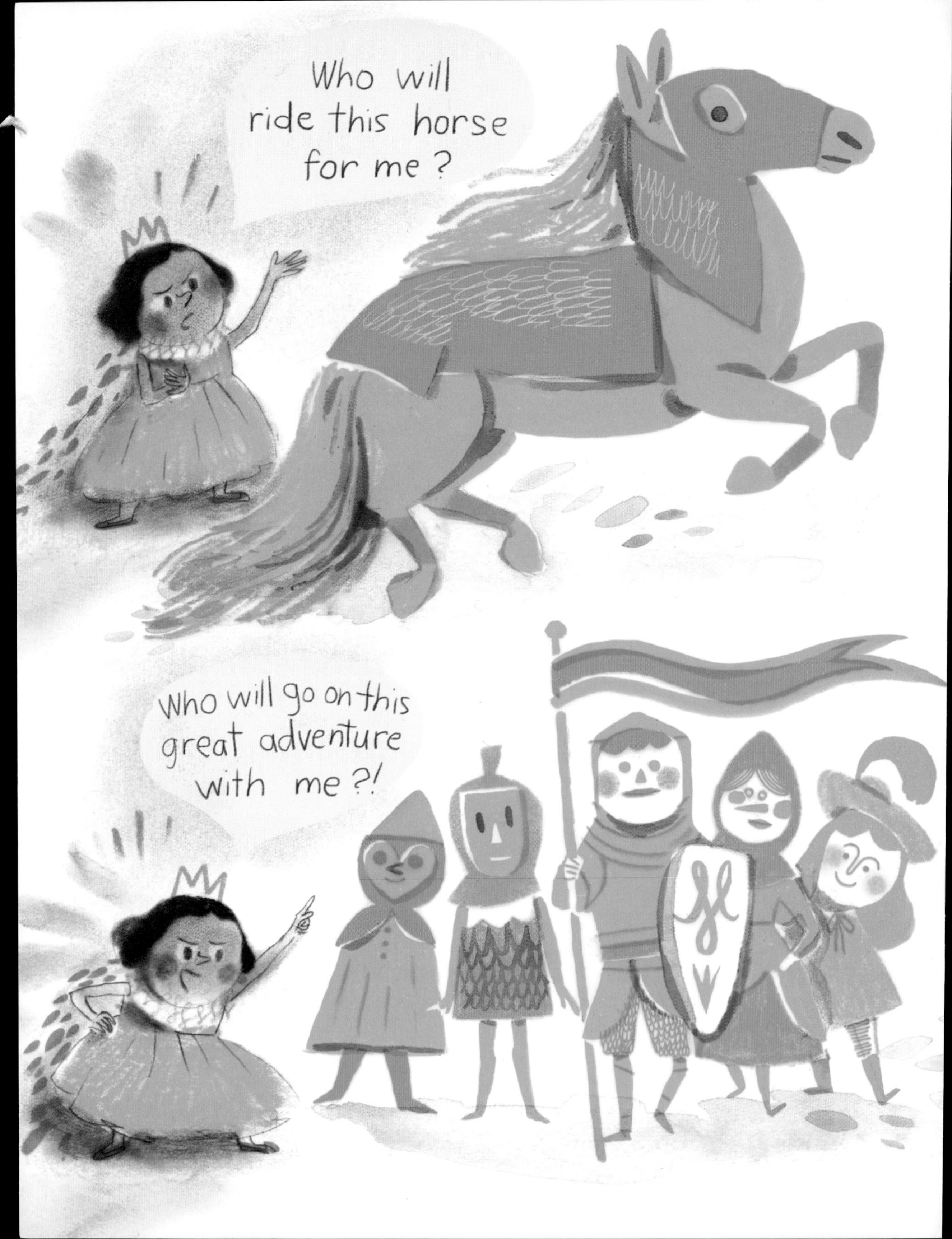
Who will ride this horse for me?
Who will go on this great adventure with me?!

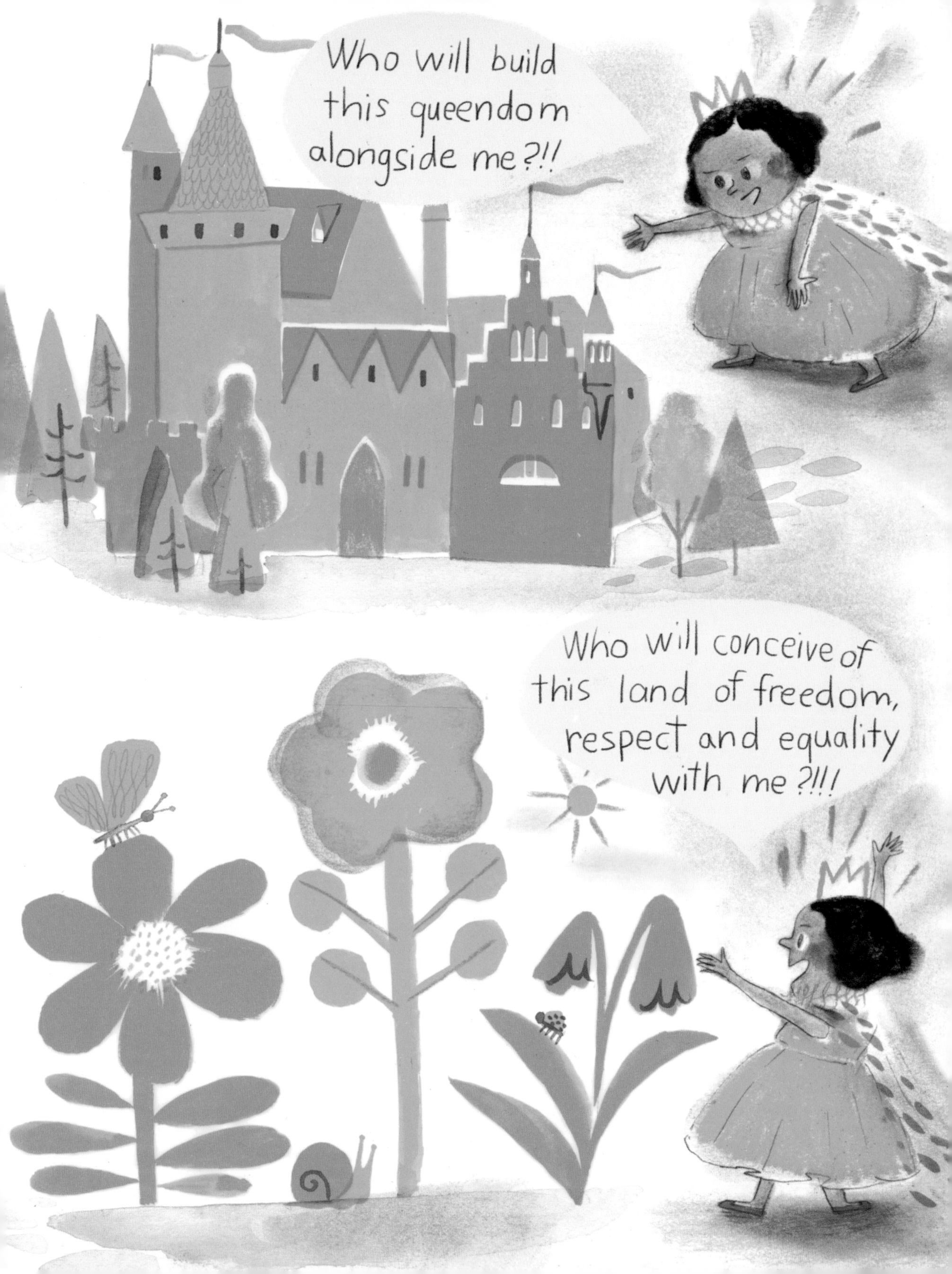
Who will build this queendom alongside me?!!
Who will conceive of this land of freedom, respect and equality with me?!!!

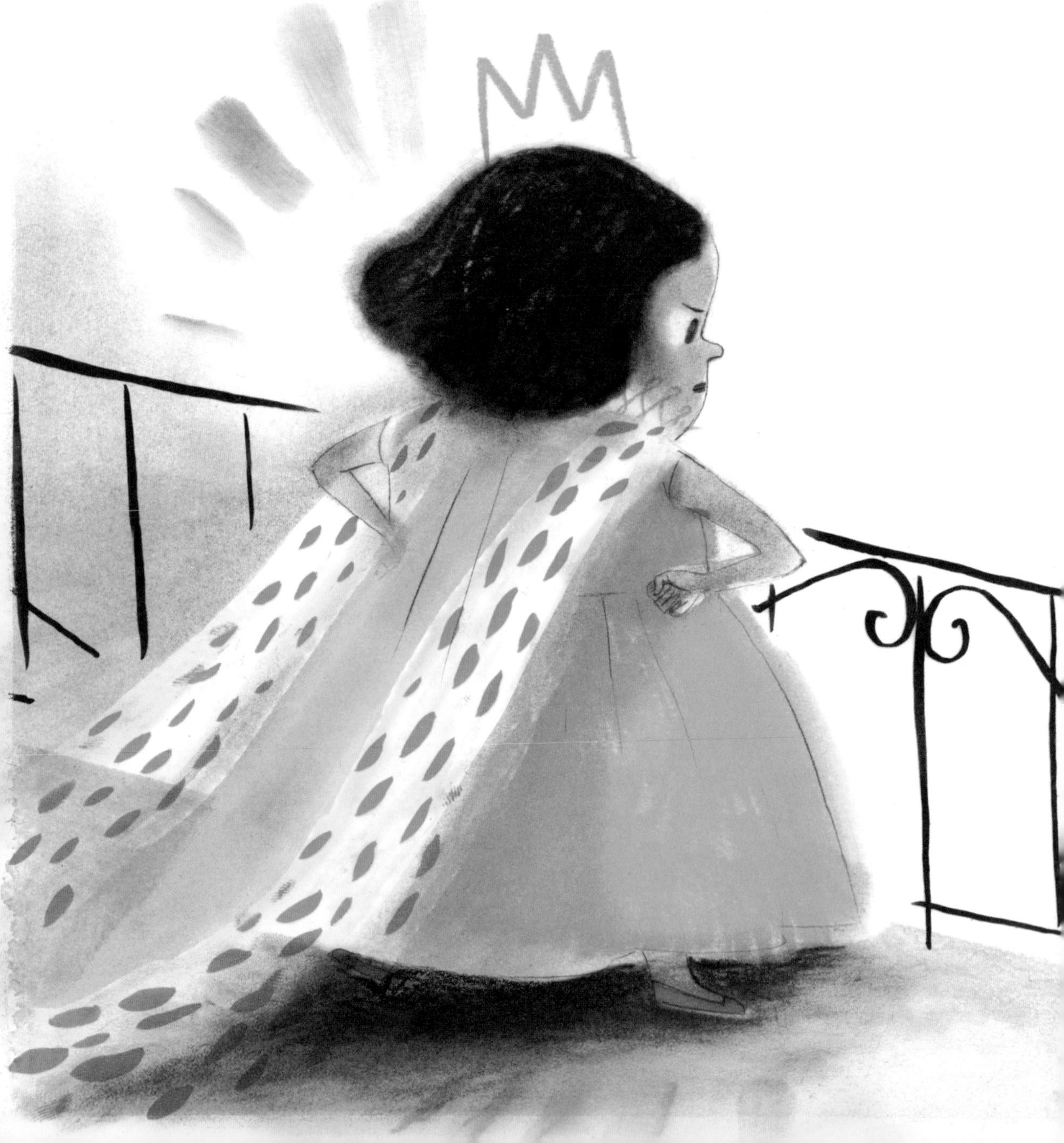

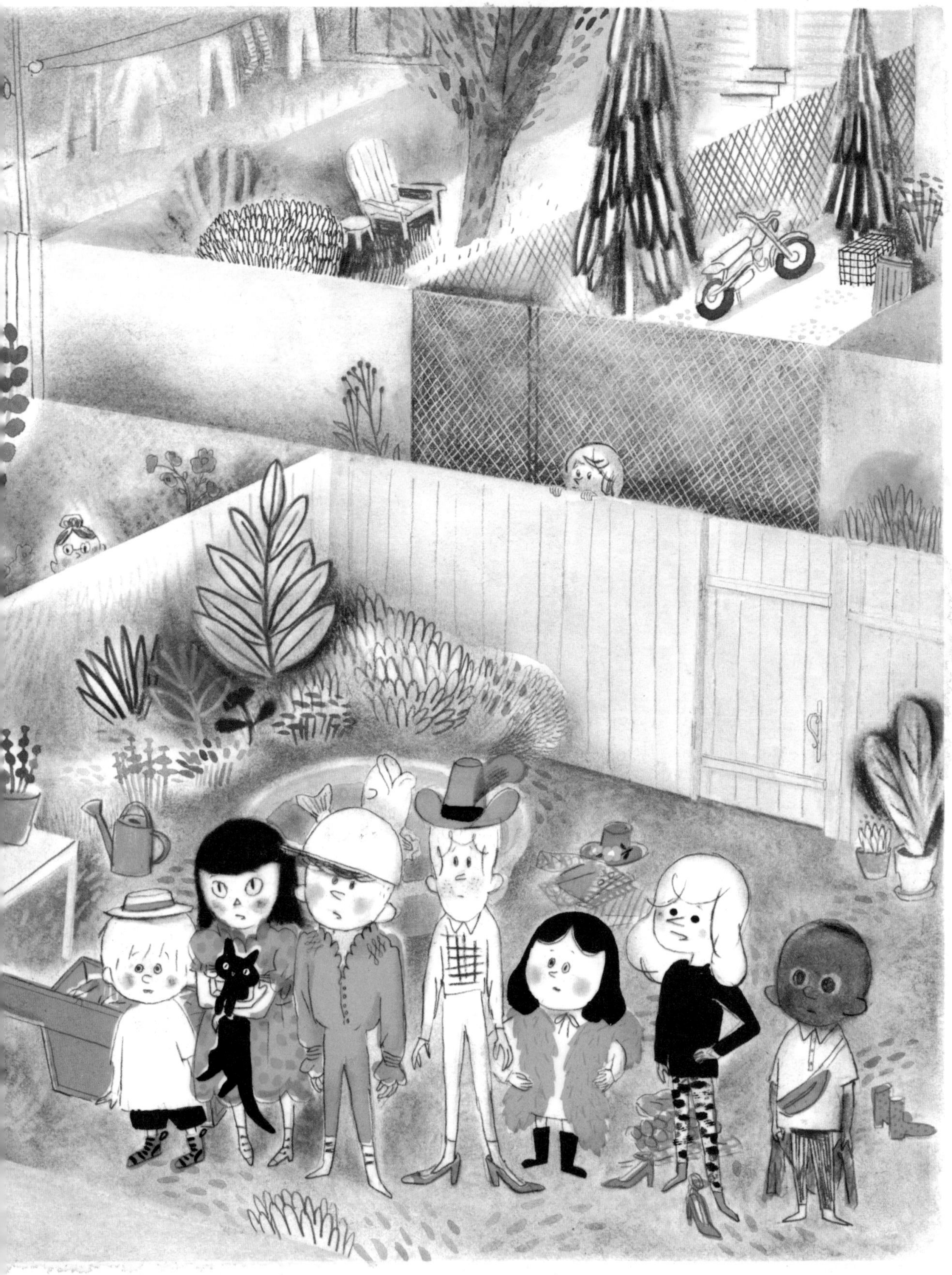

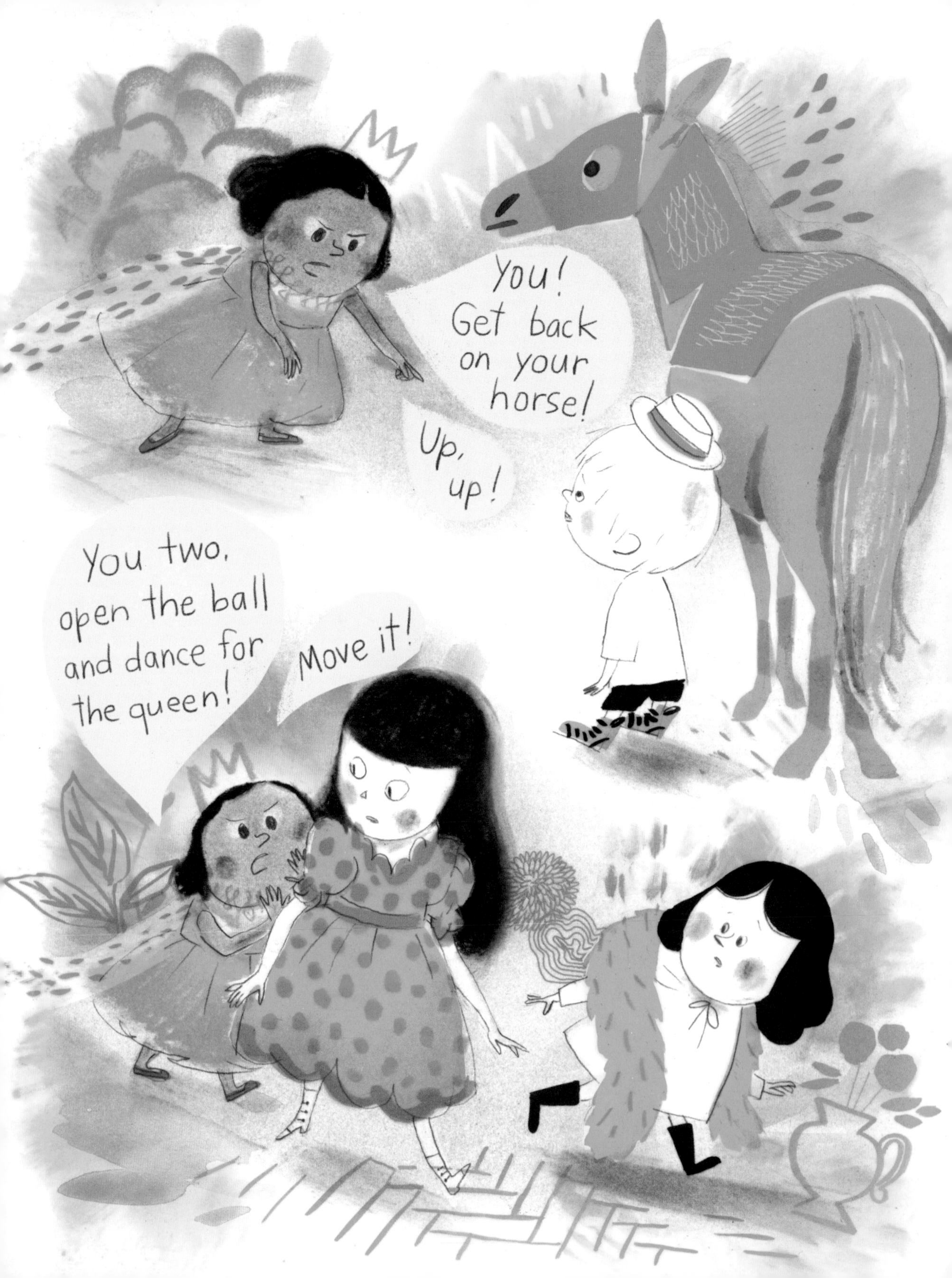
You! Get back on your horse!
Up, up!
You two, open the ball and dance for the queen!
Move it!

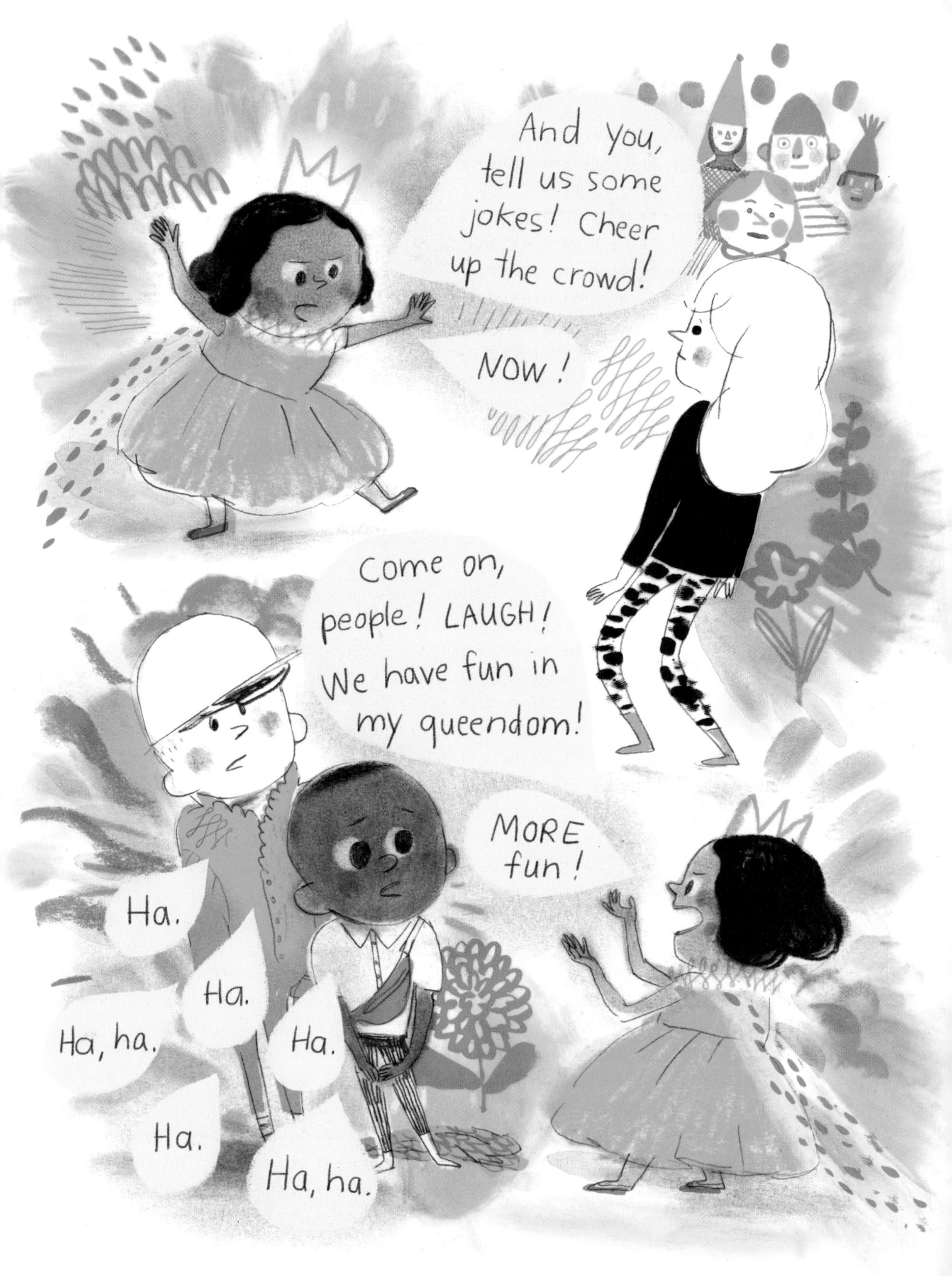
And you, tell us some jokes! Cheer up the crowd!
NOW!
Come on, people! LAUGH! We have fun in my queendom!
MORE fun!
Ha.
Ha.
Ha, ha.
Ha.
Ha.
Ha, ha.

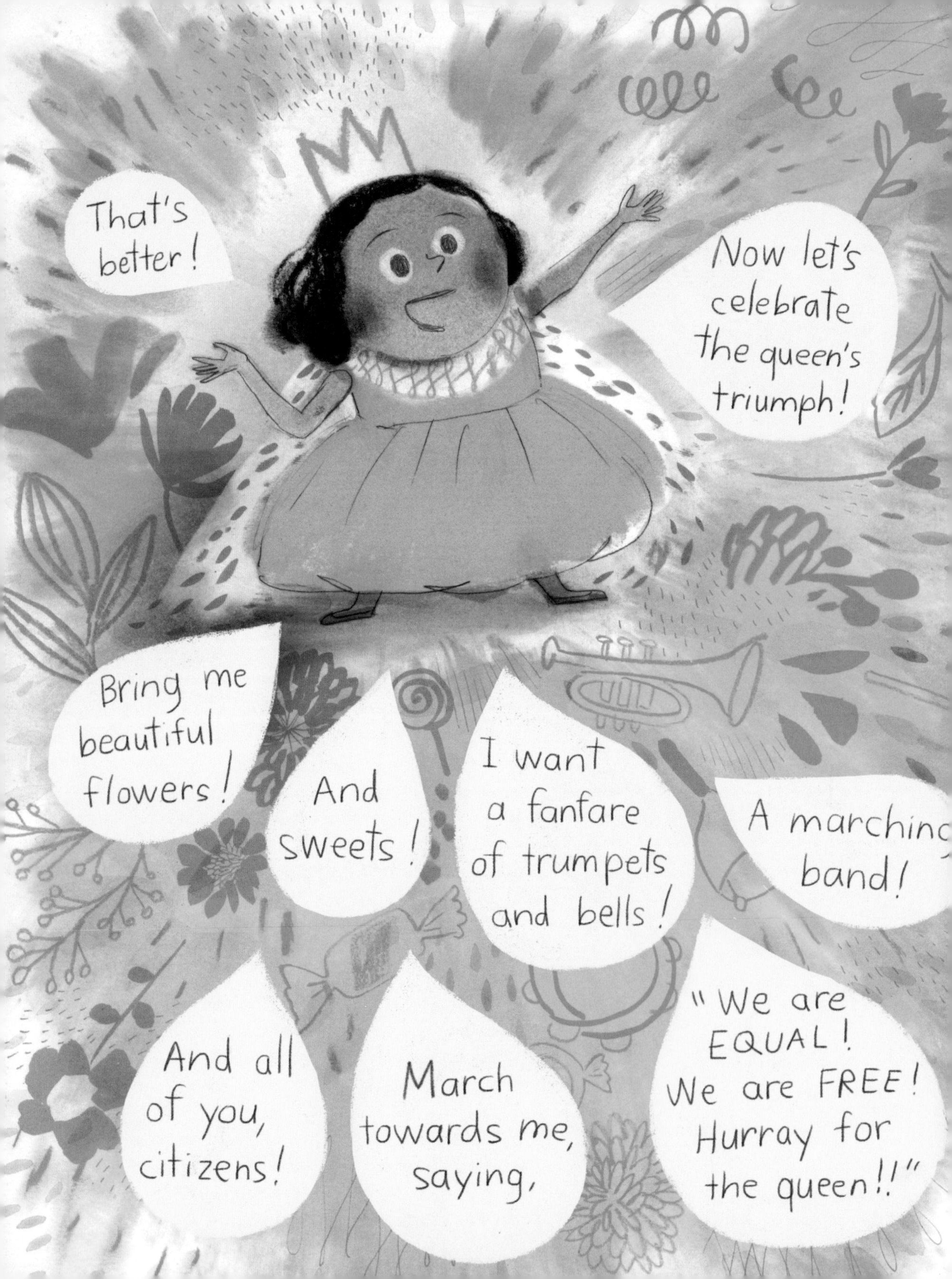
That's better!
Now let's celebrate the queen's triumph!
Bring me beautiful flowers!
And sweets!
I want a fanfare of trumpets and bells!
A marching band!
And all of you, citizens!
March towards me, saying,
"We are EQUAL! We are FREE! Hurray for the queen!!"

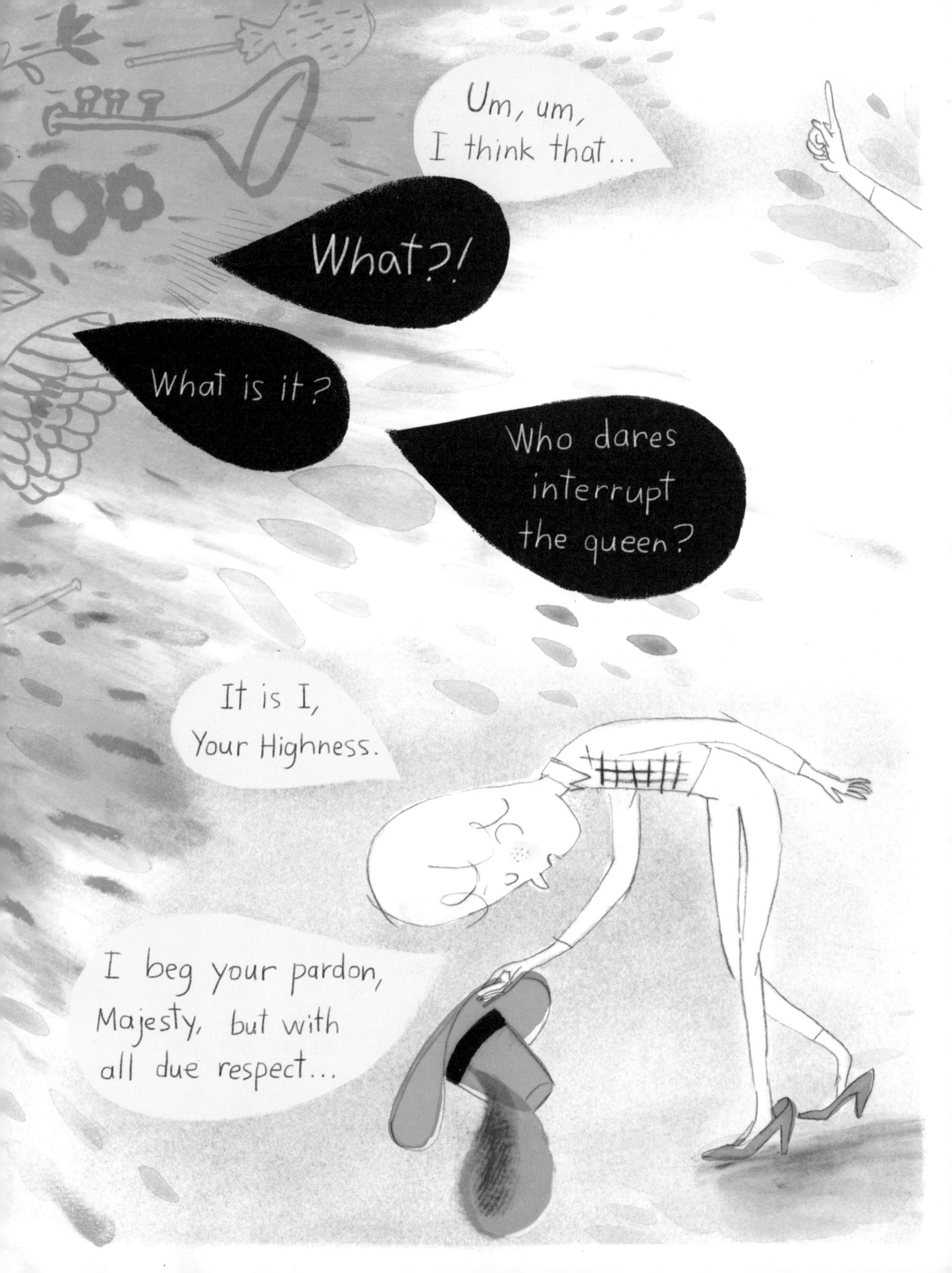

Um, um, I think that...
What?!
What is it?
Who dares interrupt the queen?
It is I, Your Highness.
I beg your pardon, Majesty, but with all due respect...

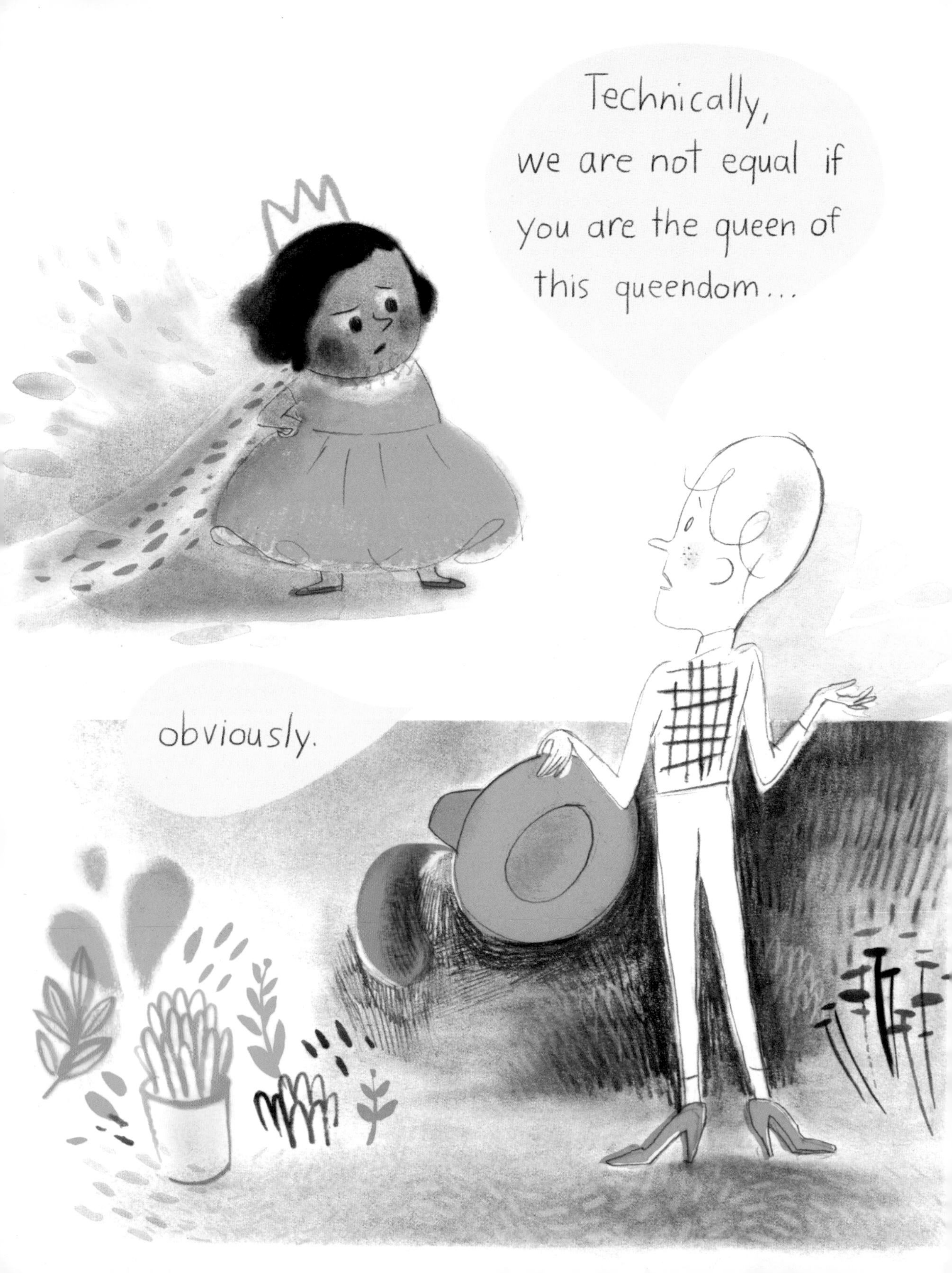
Technically, we are not equal if you are the queen of this queendom...
obviously.

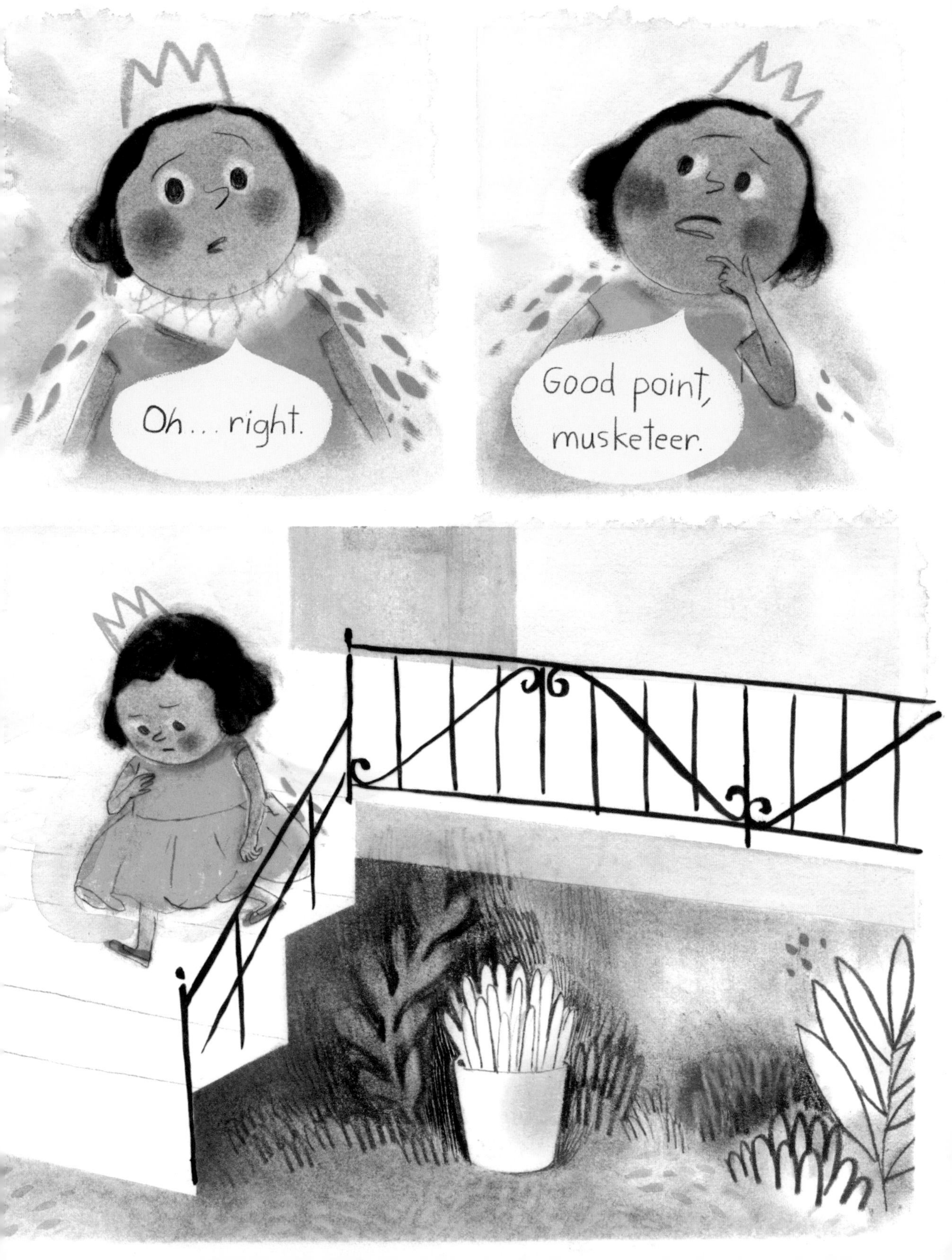
Oh... right.
Good point, musketeer.

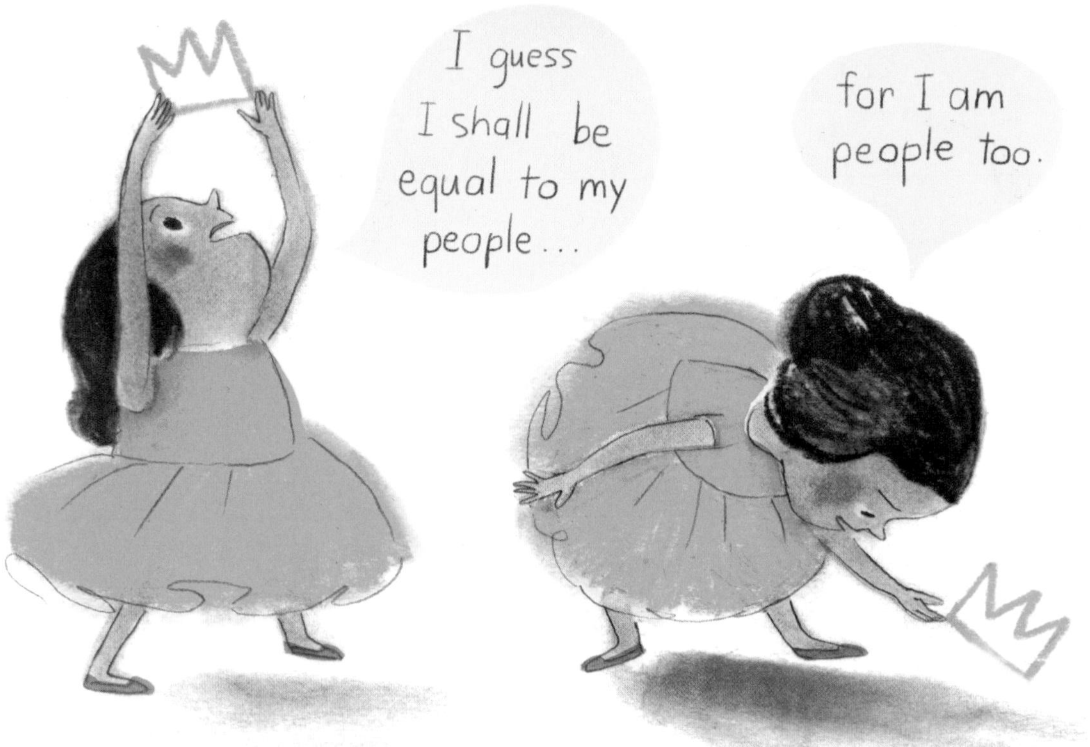
I guess I shall be equal to my people...
for I am people too.

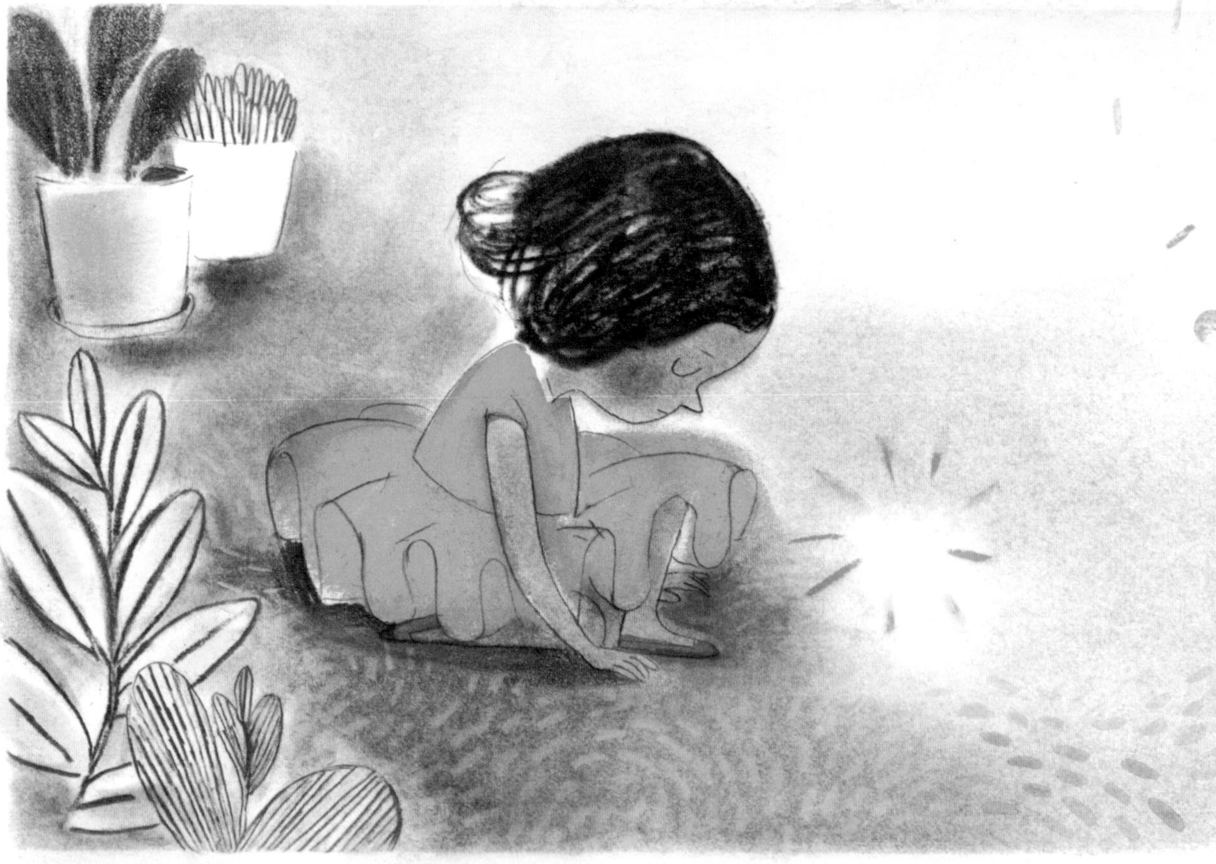

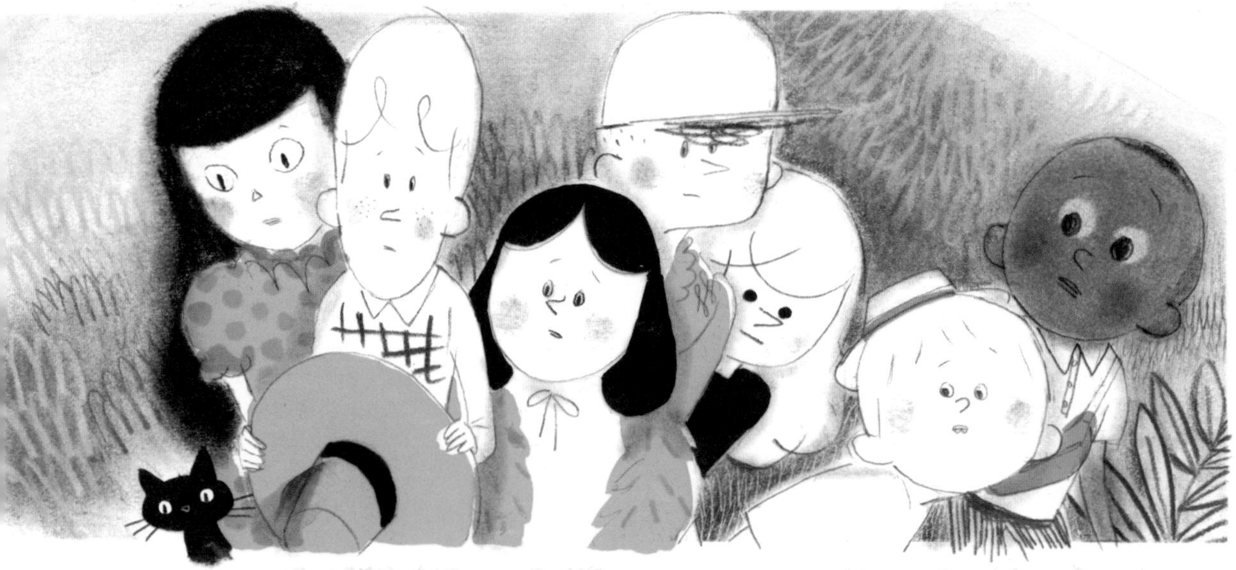
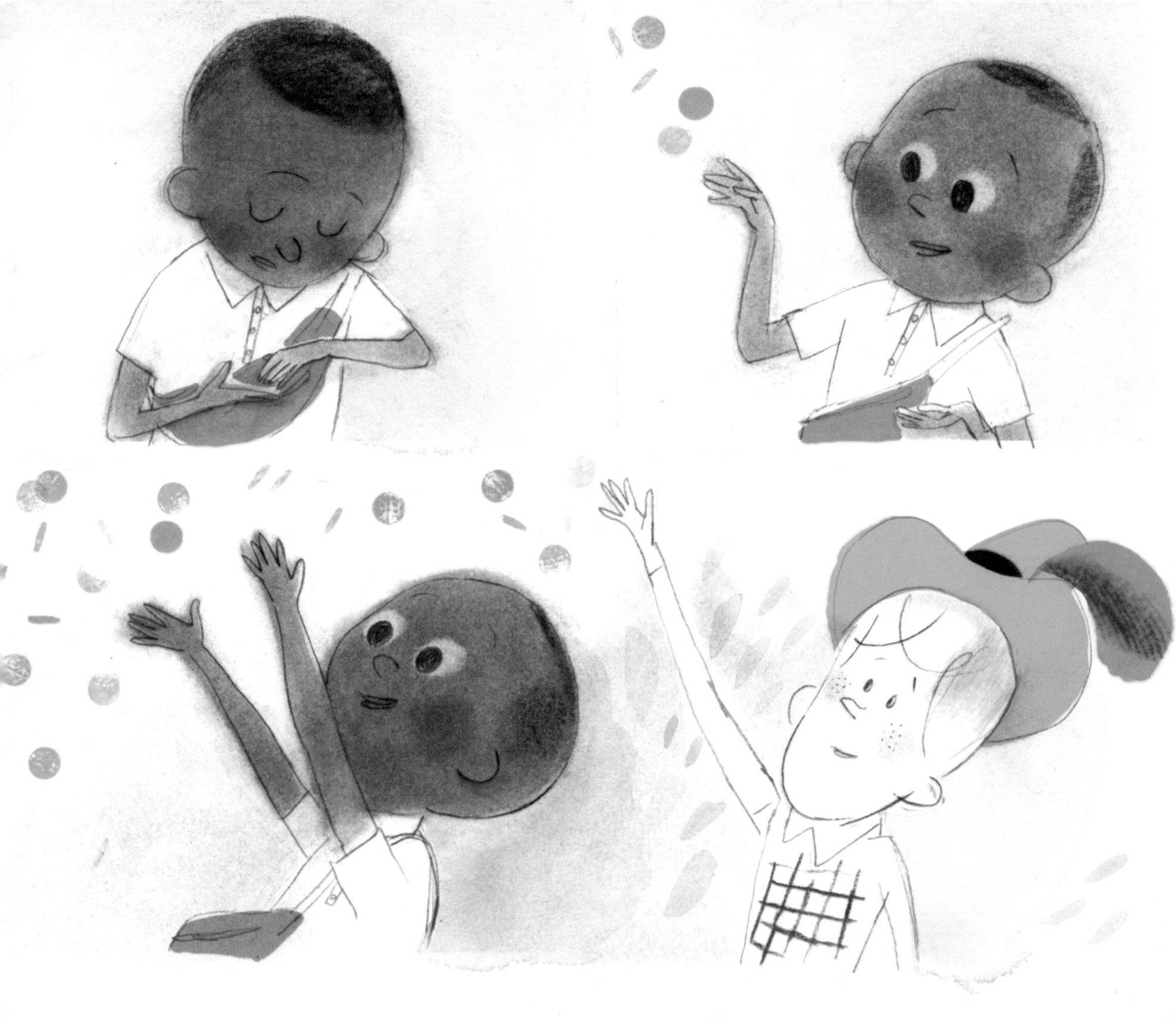

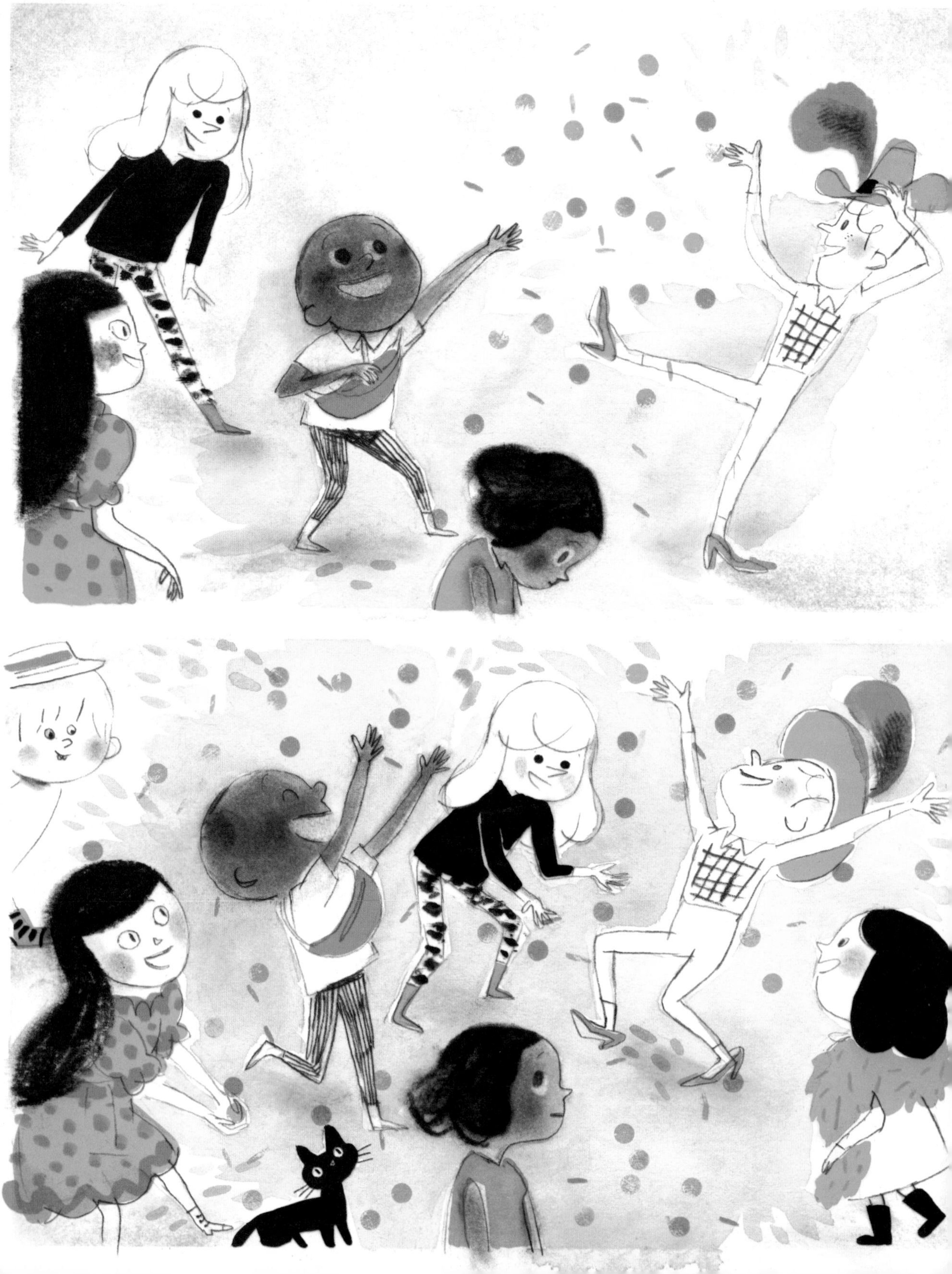

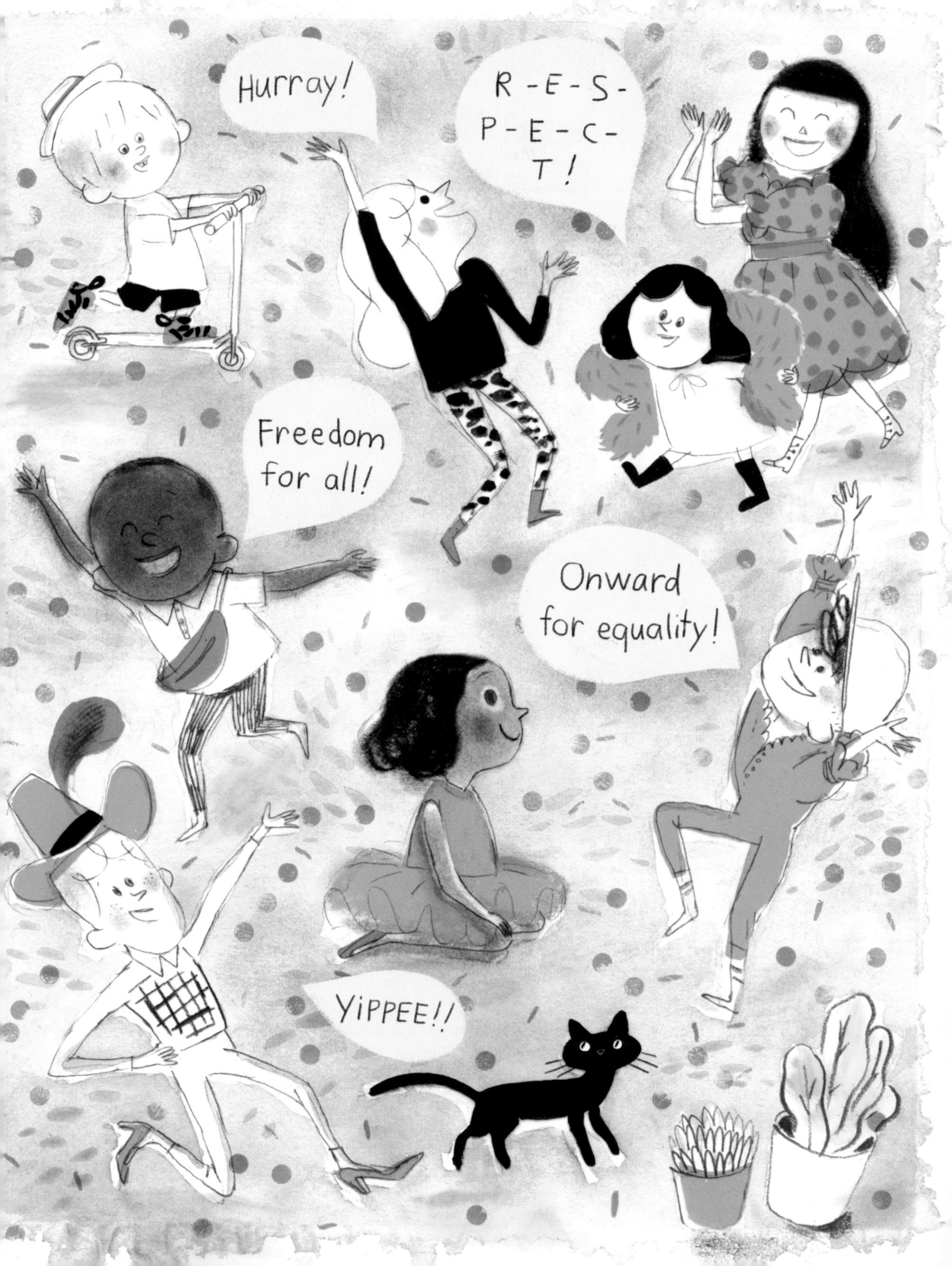
Hurray!
R-E-S-P-E-C-T!
Freedom for all!
Onward for equality!
YiPPEE!!

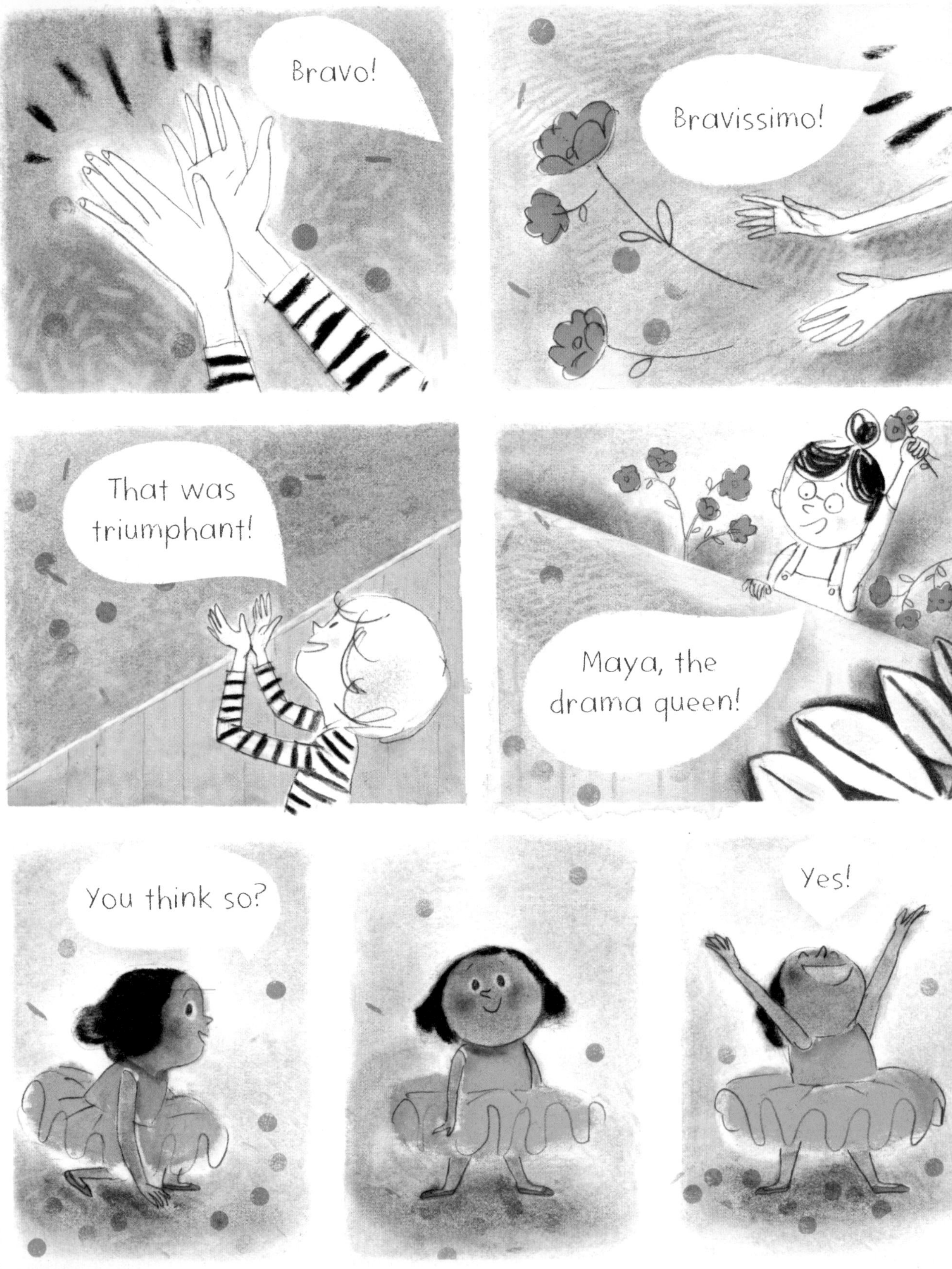
Bravo!
Bravissimo!
That was triumphant!
Maya, the drama queen!
You think so?
Yes!

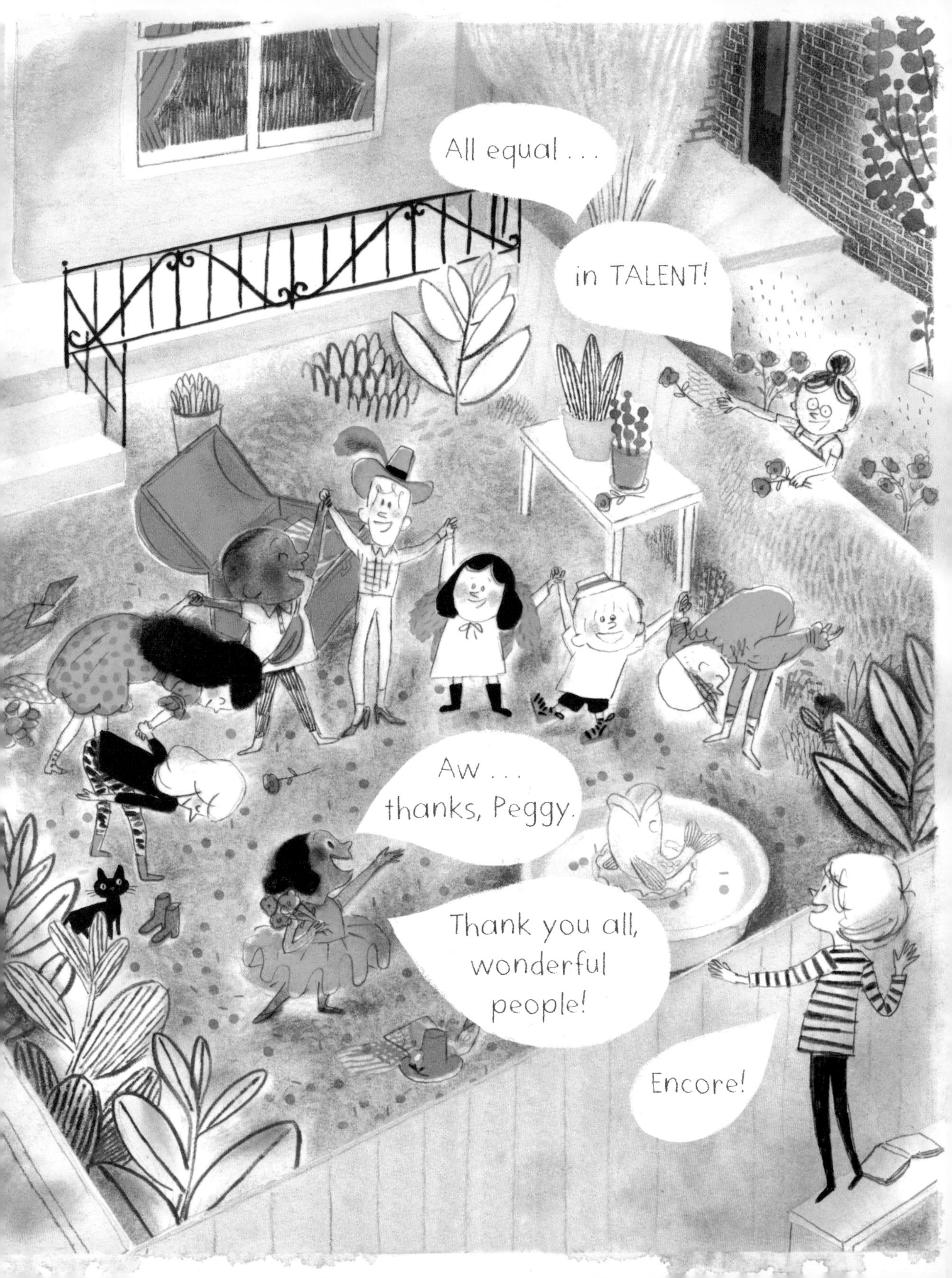
All equal . . .
in TALENT!
Aw . . .
thanks, Peggy.
Thank you all, wonderful people!
Encore!

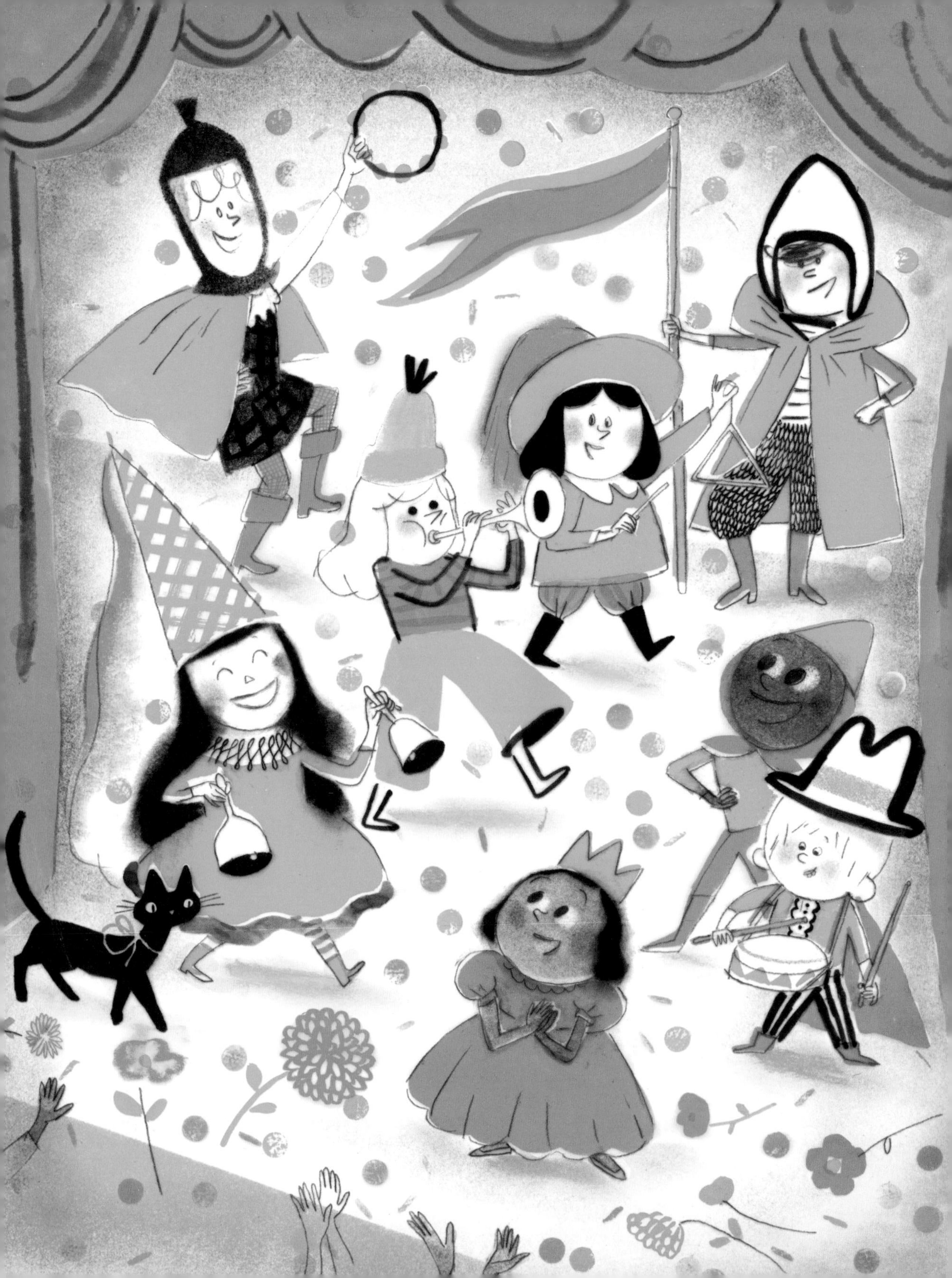

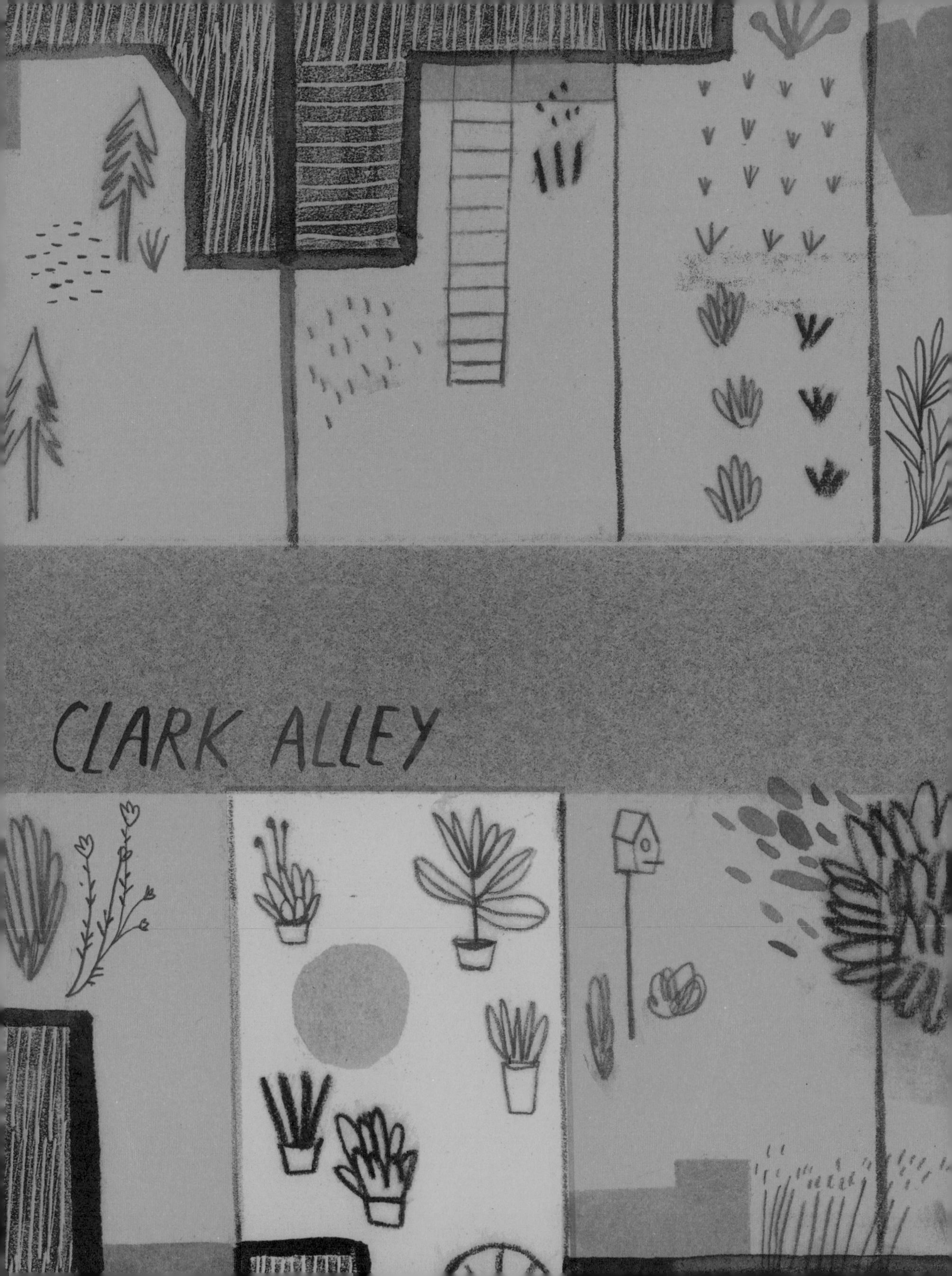
CLARK ALLEY